MW01242032

NAUGHTY
Neighbor

JEANNINE COLETTE
LAUREN RUNOW

Copyright © 2020 by Jeannine Colette and Lauren Runow. All rights reserved.

Visit our websites at www.JeannineColette.com and www.LaurenRunow.com

Cover photo credit: kiuikson

Editor: Jovana Shirley, Unforeseen Editing, www.unforeseenediting.com

Beta read by Indie Solutions, www.murphyrae.net.

No part of this book may be reproduced or transmitted in any form or by any means, electronic or mechanical, including photocopying, recording, or by any information storage and retrieval system without the written permission of the author, except for the use of brief quotations in a book review.

This book is a work of fiction. Names, characters, places, and incidents either are products of the author's imagination or are used fictitiously. Any resemblance to actual persons, living or dead, events, or locales is entirely coincidental.

No copyright infringement intended. No claims have been made over songs and/or lyrics written. All credit goes to original owners.

FALLING FOR THE STARS

A Zodiac-Themed Romance Series celebrates the unique qualities of men based on their zodiac sign. Each book features a distinctive trope, a kick-ass heroine, and a love written in the stars!

This book's hero is the *Libra*.

Romantic, Charming, Intellectual, Flirtatious, Polite, Diplomatic, Sociable, Smartly Dressed, Overly Sensitive, Indecisive.

CHAPTER ONE

He walks into the room, and there's a sinful glare to his eyes. One that makes me stop and grow weak in the knees.

"I can't want you, Tanner," I breathe.

"Why not?" His voice is a whisper, but his eyes are shouting at me in challenge, willing me to tell him why I'm fighting this urge to lean forward and kiss him.

I want to tear his clothes off his body and ride out our lust-filled attraction until we're in a sea of bliss, and yet the only words I can utter are ...

...

...

Fuck.

I have no idea what to write next.

When I decided to become a romance novelist, it was with high ideals of living the dream. Sleep late. Spend my days at leisure. Write when I was in the mood. And pump out page after page of literary magic.

Boy, how naive I was.

NAUGHTY NEIGHBOR

Don't get me wrong. I've had soaring success as Lacey Rivers, indie contemporary romance author, hitting *Amazon*'s Top 10 list twice. But now, I'm suffering from an author's worst nightmare.

Writer's block.

I look down at my laptop and the blinking cursor that's taunting me.

"You can do this, Lacey. Just get the words on the page," I say to myself as I shake my body to reinvigorate the creative juices. Then, I start to type.

"Why do you deny this feeling?" His lips nip the lobe of my ear.

"Because I don't believe in love."

He pulls back and looks down at me with a deep scowl. "How can you say such a thing?"

"I can't believe in something that doesn't exist."

Oh, for the love of Tom Hardy, even I know this is trash.

I once went to a seminar where Jodi Picoult said, "You can't edit a blank page."

That has become my motto and one I'm practicing right now. It's complete drivel, what I'm writing, I know. But I just have to get it out. Put the pen to paper.

I start again. To my surprise, I get a vision of a romantic couple in an angsty exchange, and the scene starts to unfold.

Yes. This is it!

The words are pouring out of me now. *Just let the characters guide you. Feel their—*

Boom, boom, thump!

I close my eyes in frustration. "You have got to be kidding me," I groan.

The sound of loud music coming from the shared wall of my apartment is deafening. Okay, maybe it's not *that* loud, but it's distracting as all hell. I look at the clock and see it's nine in the evening, which means this could be the start of hours of raucous partying.

Boom, boom, thump!

With a huff, I place my laptop on the couch and get up. It pains me to do so when I was finally getting lost in a scene.

That's why I love writing. Screw the real world and everything that comes along with it. Give me my laptop and a glass of wine, and when I'm not having writer's block, I can get lost in writing my next novel for hours— *boom, boom thump!*—until someone relentlessly blares music for all to hear.

I exit my apartment and walk next door. My knuckles vibrate with how hard I knock. In fact, my fist is still moving as the door opens, and I'm greeted by the devilishly handsome smile of the man who lives next door.

Jake Moreau.

"Hey, Lacey. Want to come in for a drink?"

His grin is panty-melting for sure.

I've lived next door to him for a while, and his attractiveness hasn't gone unnoticed. Lean yet muscular build, swoonworthy eyes the color of chocolate, and the perfect angle of his jaw, which is rugged and pretty, all at the same time.

Clearly, I've been preoccupied with describing my literary heroes because I'm currently spending way too

3

much time appreciating how good-looking Jake is … and not the problem at hand.

"Do you mind turning the music down? I'm trying to work."

His brows curve in concern. "Sure, but I have friends over. It's Friday night. Most people like to unwind after a long week."

"Yes, agreed. However, I don't work a conventional job, and my hours go beyond the nine to five."

He grabs the top of the doorframe and leans into it with his full mouth puckered in interest. "What are your hours?"

"I don't know. Sometimes, ten to four, and other times, noon to ten. They fluctuate." I shrug.

"Well, while you're sleeping in until ten in the morning, the rest of us have been up and are four hours into our workday."

My jaw drops as I wonder if I should be insulted or not, but then Jake lets out a loud laugh.

"I'm teasing," he says, nudging me in the shoulder. "You're so serious. If you want me to turn the music down, I will."

"Thanks. I appreciate it." I turn to leave, but he stops me.

"What do you do anyway?"

"Do?"

"For a living. The job with unconventional working hours?"

I inwardly cringe, not because I'm embarrassed of my job. In fact, I'm damn proud. I just get weary of the reaction I get from men when they learn I write sultry love stories. The response is sometimes crude.

"I'm an author." I adjust my feet in the carpeted hallway.

"Wow. That's awesome," he says, genuinely impressed. "Anything I might have heard of?"

"No. I write romance. Not something you'd be interested in."

I start to back away, but he follows me into the hall.

"What makes you think a man wouldn't read romance?"

I briefly close my eyes then open them and try to explain, "It's women's fiction."

He shrugs. "I believe in love at first sight and kisses that make your heart pound. And trust me when I say, I wouldn't blush at a sex scene."

The way his eyes smolder as he says the word *sex* sends a shiver through my body. I need to bottle his baritone and re-create it in a love scene.

His words surprise me, too, since I've seen the amount of gorgeously dressed women who come roaming in and out of his apartment. He doesn't seem like the guy who is looking for a commitment.

"Well, if you don't mind just giving me two hours, that would be awesome. Don't stop your party, just don't blast the music."

"Are you sure you don't want to come in? Not even for one drink?" he asks again, motioning toward the partly open doorway.

There has to be a dozen people inside, if not more. They're all laughing and drinking, unwinding after their long day at the office, I imagine. I'm envious of them actually. I'd kill for a drink right now and a coworker to commiserate with.

"Maybe some other time." I spin on my heel and head to my door.

As I step inside my apartment, I see Jake has already entered his own and closed the door.

Sighing, I walk around my home, past the galley kitchen that looks into the living room. I grab my laptop off the couch and walk it over to my desk by the window. The crescent-shaped moon is bright tonight. The kind that movies use when depicting dreams. It makes me smile, seeing as I have many dreams of my own that I wish to come true. My main dream is taking my career to the next level by being represented by a major publishing house. I'd become the author my mother would be proud of, and I'd have job security that would help plan for my future.

The music coming from Jake's apartment lowers, and I can hear someone audibly complain. There's still a dull roar, but I can work with that. I increase my own mood music and get back to work, biting my thumbnail as I reread my words. I'm not sold on them, and I consider rewriting the whole thing.

I'm hitting Delete when there's a knock at my door.

My eyes squint as I purse my mouth, confused as to who it could be. Since I live in a secured building, all guests have to hit the buzzer downstairs. Whoever is at my door must live in my building.

I pad over and open it to see Jake standing there with a glass in one hand, the other raking through his lustrous hair.

"Since you refuse to come over, I thought I'd bring the party to you."

I eye him curiously as he strolls in, handing me the glass of wine, and heads straight for my living room.

"Thanks," I say, closing the door even though I never told him to come in. "You didn't have to do that."

"We're neighbors. It's the kind thing to do after I annoyed you with my music."

I've lived in this building for a few years and never brought a drink to someone else's house in kindness. I'm not sociable like that. I take a sip of the wine and nod in approval.

At least he has good taste in vino.

Standing at the kitchen counter, I watch as he strolls around. My apartment is a decent size—one bedroom, full bath, kitchen, and living room/dining room combo—but add in the six-foot-tall man dressed in jeans, a pale pink button-down, and smoldering good looks, it feels claustrophobic. His presence, as well as his honey-scented cologne, lingers in every square inch of the place.

"These your books?" He points to the bookcase near my desk.

"Yep. I keep a lot of extras for people who order signed copies."

He whistles through his teeth as he takes in the rows of paperbacks. "That's impressive. Let me buy one off of you."

I shake my head. "No need. Just grab one."

"Any suggestions?"

I roll my eyes. It's not like he's actually gonna read it, so I walk over and pick the first book I see. It's called *Fire and Gold*, and it was my first best seller.

He holds it in his hands, feeling the weight of it.

"This is quite the accomplishment. Your parents must be proud."

Proud isn't the word I'd use.

"Of course."

"You hesitated."

I brush him off. "She is satisfied with my career."

His eyes narrow, as if he's trying to decide if I'm lying or not. An attuned man is a dangerous one, as they can read between the lines.

"I'll let you know what I think of this." He holds up the book and looks at the cover with the shirtless model glowering with searing intensity. "Nice abs."

"Did you come here to borrow a book?" I ask with an unsure smile.

He grins. "Kind of. I just wanted to bring you the wine and see what life was like on the other side of the wall. You've never knocked on my door before."

"I most definitely have. When you moved in, I came over to introduce myself. You answered while wearing nothing but a seafoam-green towel, and a woman, who looked to have on the previous night's clothes, came strolling out."

His brows go up. The smile on his face grows devilish as he tucks the book under his arm. "What kind of dress was she wearing?"

I blanch at his ridiculous question. "I have absolutely no idea. Why would it matter?"

He takes five steps forward, closing the space between us. My shoulders push back on instinct, and my chin rises. His cocky stature hovers above me as he looks down, making my heart race.

"You remembered what I was wearing but not the woman?"

"It was a green towel. Hardly a detail difficult to remember."

"A *seafoam*-green towel," he says as he saunters past me and toward the door, stopping to open it and glancing back. "Offer still stands. Come over if you need a break."

The door closes behind him, and I let out the breath I was holding since he uttered the word *seafoam*. It's not even a sexy word, and yet the way he said it, like it was the code word to his secret lair, has me falling to my couch with my hand over my eyes, wondering why I'd had to go and knock on my neighbor's door tonight.

Because he was playing loud music. Which he turned down and then brought me a glass of wine.

Either Jake is the nicest person on the planet or evil incarnate in Ferragamo shoes, trying to butter me up.

Well, I guess one thing was accomplished tonight. I can, without a doubt, confirm the hero on my pages is a dud because I'm more inspired by the words from the man next door than the fictitious one I'm currently trying to create.

CHAPTER TWO

"Auntie!" The pitter-patter of baby girl feet comes from the hallway.

"There's my Bree Bree!" I place my purse on the entryway table and pick up my favorite girl, squeezing her tightly as I kiss her cheek.

"*Wook* at my *dow-ee*," she tells me, holding up a toy I haven't seen before. This one is a baby doll with pink hair and purple eyes, wearing leopard-print pajamas.

"Why, this is the sweetest baby I've ever seen. Is she new?"

Aubrey dramatically nods her head before hugging it, closing her eyes, and loving on her new toy.

"Looks like my favorite little lady has been a good girl," I say as I tickle her belly.

Her laughter is the best sound I've ever heard.

The toddler is giggling and squirming in my arms as her mom—and my best friend—Charisse walks into the hall while wiping her hands on a rag.

NAUGHTY NEIGHBOR

"Don't let that tiny ball of sunshine fool you. She's a house-wrecker. This morning, she took my lipsticks and made a mural on the bathroom wall," Charisse says, giving her daughter a stern expression.

My eyes pop with surprise as I try to hide my laugh when I turn to my goddaughter. "Aubrey Claire, you do not use Mommy's makeup for art. You'll ruin the walls—and Mommy's expensive gloss. If anyone is going to waste it, it's going to be me."

Aubrey's lip pops out with a pout. I hold her closer, shushing her in comfort before she cries.

"You know, when you tell a child she's done something wrong, it's usually not followed by a hug," Charisse says with a grin.

I wave her off. "I can't stand to see her little lip. It's the saddest—and cutest—thing in the world," I explain. "Besides, I'm the fun aunt. Your job is to ground her, and mine is to be the shoulder to lean on, so she can talk about how awful her mother is."

Charisse whips my butt with the dishtowel in her hand. "Just make sure you let me know on the sly when she eventually comes to you, talking about boys, sex, and smoking pot."

I cover Aubrey's ear with my hand and bring her head to my chest to cover the other ear. "Don't let my sweet girl hear you speak of such things," I say sarcastically.

Charisse is laughing while her wife, Melody, walks into the room.

"Hey, Lacey. You're just in time for drinks."

"Sounds good." I follow the ladies into the living room.

Charisse and Melody have the kind of home people aspire to create. Located in the western suburbs of Chicago, their house is a Tudor style with wood-beamed ceilings and large black-paned windows. One look around reveals wall upon wall of family photos, many of them black-and-whites of their parents, grandparents, and themselves growing up.

If there ever were a home that told a tale, it is this one. And this home is about love, especially when you see the picture frames on table after table of their baby, who entered their world three years ago.

I put Aubrey down on the floor in her toy corner, and she immediately starts playing with her doll, putting her in a cradle and rocking her to sleep. I pat her silky black hair and give her a kiss.

On the coffee table is a photo of Charisse and me, taken about six years ago. She was the first friend I made when I moved to the city. We were working at a production company when we hit it off as great friends. Fast-forward a few years later, she told me she was sick of waiting for the perfect woman to come around and wanted to have a baby on her own. Being a mother was the only thing Charisse had ever dreamed of, and she didn't want to put it off for another moment. I gave her my support and my time, even meeting her during her lunch breaks to give her hormone shots for her fertility treatments.

Two months into the pregnancy, she met Melody. Not only did Melody not care that this fabulous woman she was falling in love with was pregnant, but she also wanted to be part of the journey. They married a year later, and the rest is history.

NAUGHTY NEIGHBOR

"Wine or water?" Melody asks as I take a seat on one of the barstools around the oversize island that separates the kitchen from the living room.

"It's always one or the other, huh?"

"The drink tells us what's really going on in that head of yours." She winks, and Charisse gives an agreeable shrug.

"Vino it is." I give in with a mock motion for her to make it a heavy pour, and the two women laugh.

While Melody pours, Charisse sets out a tray of meat and cheese. "What are your troubles, Miss Rivers?"

"The words aren't coming, and the ones that do all suck."

Melody tops off a glass for me and then pours a second tall one for herself.

Charisse leans over and looks at the pour with exaggerated eyes. "You having writer's block, too, Mel?" she teases.

"I"—Melody places her hand on her chest—"am being a good friend who doesn't leave another friend to drown in her sorrows alone."

"Oh, okay. So, I take it, I'll be making dinner while you two sorrow it up?" Charisse shakes her head.

"Sounds good," Melody responds as we clink glasses.

"For the record, she's my friend. No stealing." Charisse smiles as she opens the fridge and takes out a brick of Pecorino Romano.

"No fighting, ladies. There's plenty of my crazy to go around. Here, give me the cheese, and I'll grate it for you." I reach over the counter in offer to help.

Charisse hands me the brick, grater and a glass bowl. "I've been with you since you published your first book, and I've never known you to have a problem with telling a story."

Melody agrees, "That's right. The two of us are always amazed at how you create these worlds and story lines. It's like we want to crawl into your head and be a part of the brilliance."

I give her a kind smile. "Says the woman who is a brilliant attorney. I want to be in *your* head for a day."

Melody cheers glasses with me again, which has us both taking another sip.

With the brick of cheese in my hand, I start to run it over the sharp edges of the grater. "I think I'm just inside my head too much with this series. The first book was a huge success, and then the second book became an instant best seller. I have readers emailing me nonstop, saying how much they love these novels and that they can't wait for the conclusion. This morning, a woman messaged me to say she is taking the day off of work on release day because she's that excited to read the final installment. There's so much pressure for this story to top the first two that I feel like my head is going to explode."

Charisse leans on the counter. "You got this, Lacey. You're an award-winning writer. The first two books came so easily to you. What makes this one different?"

I sigh before looking up at them. "I think I'm running out of ideas."

Melody laughs. "No way. With that imagination of yours? You could write for a hundred years and still surprise the hell out of us."

"It's like I can't picture the guy in my head. I don't know who he is yet. What his quirks or mannerisms are. I don't even know if he likes wine or whiskey." I go back to grating, frustrated and taking it out on the cheese.

Charisse takes the brick and grater from me. "Okay, we only need enough to put on our salads. We're not making a lasagna here."

I chuckle under my breath as I drop my chin to my chest. "Why is my brain on lockdown?"

"Maybe it's because you haven't actually been on a date in eons. Have you thought about that?" Charisse asks as she puts the cheese away, taking out the romaine. "When was the last time you went on a date?"

I blow her off. "I've been on plenty. To a gala at an art museum, dinner on a rooftop in San Francisco—"

"Those were fictional dates in your books. When was the last time *you* went out with a *real* man?"

I grab my glass, almost too embarrassed to answer. "Not since Michael."

Melody's jaw drops as she looks at her wife, who nods in a knowing way and turns to me sympathetically.

"Honey, the asshole left five years ago. No wonder you're running out of ideas. You have nothing to spark your imagination," she says.

I purse my lips. "I read books and watch movies. Plus, I watch my couple friends. I have plenty of inspiration," I explain.

"Why don't you let me set you up with Tommy? He's a good-looking guy and a successful accountant," Melody suggests.

"Oh, he's cute. Lacey, he's totally your type. Thick, dark hair and these amazing hazel-greens. The whole package," Charisse says with a glimmer to her eye.

"You are not hooking me up with a finance guy," I deadpan.

"Hey, there's nothing wrong with a businessman. Hell, you're always writing them as these hot dominants in the bedroom. Shit, he might even be able to save you some money with those crazy-ass quarterly taxes you have to pay." Melody nods while pointing at me with her glass in hand.

I shake my head and take a gulp. "You know, I've always considered you my favorite couple because you've never tried to set me up with someone. It's as if the world can't handle a twenty-eight-year-old woman without a love interest."

Charisse pauses her chopping and tilts her head while resting the knife on the counter. Her expression has just morphed from best friend to concerned mother. "You can't stay single forever. It's been *five* years. I get it. I was there when Michael left and fucked up your world, but that was just one guy. I swear there are good ones out there. Don't turn into your mother."

The problem with having close friends is you let them into all aspects of your life. Even the parts you don't want to talk about.

I've been content these past five years, living my life the way I want. I like not having to answer to anyone, and I don't need a man to make me happy. Yes, my mom hasn't dated anyone since my dad walked out on us, but that's her choice. And this is mine.

I try to lighten the mood by laughing when I say, "Coming from the girl who's never liked guys."

Charisse throws a strip of lettuce at me. "Totally

different, and you know it. I just hate seeing you not even trying to get back out there."

I play with my glass, pretending to think about it even though I'm not really. I have no interest in dating. Not anymore. My book boyfriends are all I need. This one just isn't talking to me yet. I know he will eventually.

Melody nudges me and says with a sweet tone, trying to lift up the mood, "Come on. You'll like Tommy. He's really sweet, and he totally understands what it's like to have a broken heart. His girlfriend walked out on him last year. I have his number. I can set you guys up."

It's not that I haven't ever wanted to meet someone and fall in love. Being married and having children have always been the end goal for me. I *love* love, and I love children even more. It's just hard to explain to others who are living the blissful life how I feel about the possibility of experiencing heartache again.

A telephone rings in the distance, and I realize it's coming from my cell phone in the foyer. I jump out of my seat, anxious to get out of this conversation of a potential blind date.

Taking my phone out of my purse, I see *Wendy Walcott*—my agent—on the screen. Ninety percent of our conversations happen over text or email, so the fact that she's calling me at seven on a Saturday night is not a good sign.

"Hi, Wendy."

"So," she sings out, "how's it going?"

"Everything's good. Really good. The manuscript is coming along," I say, sliding my hand in my jeans pocket.

Then, I hear Charisse cough out from the kitchen, "Liar."

I walk around the corner to give her the evil eye, and they both laugh, so I walk back down the hall to get some privacy.

"That's awesome because I have huge news for you. I've been shopping you around to a bunch of publishing houses. Winston Arms just returned my call, and their editor read your books and is loving this series. She said they're looking for a new author to sign on, and she thinks you might be a perfect fit for their readers."

My hand flies to my mouth as I take in the magnitude of this moment. Winston Arms is one of the premier publishing houses in the country with an imprint dedicated to the romance genre. Anyone who signs with them becomes an instant *New York Times* best seller.

"Oh my God, Wendy, this is huge!"

"Honey, this is beyond huge. If you sign with them, you're talking a massive signing bonus and royalties that will make you drool."

I pump my fist in the air as the excitement builds up in my body, making my eyes well up. Being a self-published author has been amazing, but I've been dreaming about being signed to a publishing house. I could extend my reader base and get my books on the shelves of bookstores.

"What's the next step? Do they want to meet me?" I ask.

"They want to *read* you. They're looking to sign you to a three-book deal, but all is contingent on how you close out this series. If you can outsell the first two books in the series and show you have the stamina, then they'll sign you on the spot. I told them that's a no-brainer. Talked you up big time. I said I've already seen the pages and that the writing is brilliant. Now, don't make a liar out of me. When can I see the first half of the book? Can you get it to me by the end of the month?"

I inhale a sharp breath and pull on my bottom lip. If I thought disappointing my readers was giving me writer's block, this monumental moment—in which my entire career is riding on—is sending me into writer's *shock.*

"Three weeks? I don't think I can—"

"Girl, this is the big leagues. They're looking for a writer who can do the work and do it fast."

Fast. Well, I have always thrived under pressure. Maybe this is the boost I need.

"Sure. Yeah, I can make that happen." It's a lie. There's no way I can get forty thousand words out by the end of the month. Maybe if I had a story, but right now, it feels impossible.

"I'm so excited for you! I know it's crazy to call on a weekend, but I just had to let you know. I can't wait to read this one. The youngest brother has been such an enigma in the first two books. I loved the secrecy of him, and I can't wait to see what you have planned."

I smack my palm to my forehead.

He was an enigma because I didn't know who he was either.

"Yep, you're going to love him. He's the best yet," I lie through my teeth.

"Great! Okay, well, I'll let you get back to your writing. Have a good night."

"You too." I hang up and drop my head to my chest.

When I walk back into the kitchen, Charisse and Melody are staring at me with a mixture of excitement and curiosity, wondering what my phone call was about.

While I want to laugh—and cry—about the opportunity that is within arm's reach, I throw my hands up and declare, "I'm so screwed."

CHAPTER THREE

Another day passes, and I have a document with only five thousand words total. Sadly, most of it is a recap about the first two books in case someone jumps in now and hasn't read the previous two. It's total crap because no one wants to open a book and reread old stories. I'm resorting to bad habits in storytelling, and I know it.

I've written six books in my short writing career, and I've never had writer's block like this.

I've tried everything to get out of it.

My day started with music while I cleaned my kitchen. Often, if I do something mindless, like scrub the floors, I can clear my head, and ideas come to me like magic. After my entire apartment was spotless, I still had no clear picture of who this guy was going to be.

I tried going for a jog, and then I tried centering myself with yoga. Neither helped.

NAUGHTY NEIGHBOR

As I hopped in the shower, I was sure the premise would come to me. I've had my most amazing plots pop in my head while I lathered shampoo through my hair. Not today though. I stood there until the water was cold and my freshly shaved legs were getting goose bumps from the shivers running over my body.

With my coziest writing clothes on and my hair in a high, slick bun, I light a candle and decide I need to immerse myself in research.

Authors are always posting about how if their computers were ever stolen, people would be sure they were serial killers. It's true. In my career, I've looked up *how to pull off the perfect murder*, *unique sex positions*, and *how to commit money laundering*. Us authors need to make sure there are no holes in our plots, and the dark World Wide Web leads the way.

I open my browser, like I have a million times before, except, today, I'm not searching how to hide crimes. I'm looking for bad porn—the kind that actually has a story line that most people will fast-forward through to get to the good stuff. Not me though. I'm dying for any twists or turns that could spark an idea.

Two hours of watching horrible acting, and I still have nothing and am beyond irritated.

I'm searching through photos of Tom Hardy, who is my physical-feature muse, when there's a knock on the door.

Whoever is there had better watch out because they're about to get the brunt of my frustration.

I look through the peephole and see the impossibly handsome face of my neighbor.

I swing the door open with more might than I probably should. My eyebrows are raised, and my hand is on my hip.

"There you go, interrupting my work hours again," I announce.

"Damn, you really know how to make a guy feel wanted," Jake says in a roguish reply as he strolls in my apartment.

I roll my eyes and drop my arms to my sides as I close the door and follow him into the kitchen.

He leans against my counter as he takes an olive from my snack dish and pops one in his mouth. "It's past ten. Office hours are closed."

"Nonconventional job, remember? I can't just clock out when the bell rings."

"That's the reason people dream for careers like yours—so they aren't slaves to their desks when they should be out, partying."

"What makes you think I don't have hot plans tonight?" I ask with a defiant crossing of my arms.

He's smirking as he stares at my yoga pants and oversize sweatshirt while he looks amazing in his slacks and button-down.

"Do you?" He raises his eyebrows in question.

"I'm on a deadline, and I've finally connected with my characters. I can't desert them now," I lie.

"Ah, another fictional boyfriend. Who's your hero? Let me guess. A charismatic thirty-year-old florist from Chicago?" he asks wistfully, like he's talking about himself.

"Nice try." I laugh off his idea as I round the kitchen island. "Wait, you're a florist?"

"Moreau Flowers, fourth generation. You sound surprised."

"A little."

He doesn't seem to be bothered by this as he continues, "At least tell me your literary hero has dirty-blond hair and chocolate-brown eyes that make you melt."

Yep, he's describing himself.

"Readers like their men to have dark hair and blue eyes."

"That's bullshit."

"It's the truth. I polled my Facebook group, and it was practically unanimous. You're not their type."

It's a lie. Based on looks alone, Jake is every woman's type. If I were to write him into a book, I'd say he was an Adonis of a man. With his chiseled jaw, full lips, fit physique, and a smile that gleams from his eyes, women become weak in the knees with just a glance. His charm and wit would make a woman fall in love instantly.

All, except for me.

"Admit it, Lace, I'm everyone's type. And before you make a joke about how conceited I am, what I mean to say is, I'm a people-pleaser. Diplomatic. Tactful. I'm a total catch."

"You mean, catch and release."

His eyes squint as he looks over at me suspiciously since a neighbor knows more than anyone else about the comings and goings from a home. "Clever."

When I moved into this building, he was the first person I met. Sure, he was standing in the hallway, wearing a towel around his waist and saying good-bye to a woman who looked like she'd slept over after their first date, but he was welcoming and cordial, even inviting me in for a welcome-to-the-building drink. I refused, of course, because no sane woman follows a half-naked man into his apartment. He appeared a few nights later, asking for sugar. I told him that sounded like a bad introduction to a porno.

I glance at the clock and sigh. "What are you doing here anyway?

"I need lime. The woman who owns the yoga studio next to the flower shop swung by to talk cross promotion. She wants a cosmopolitan, and I'm out of citrus."

"A rather intimate and late business meeting, don't ya think?" I say with a knowing grin as I walk to the refrigerator.

He levels his gaze at me. "You're judging."

"What is there to judge? Other than the fact that she drinks cosmos when Manhattans are the superior drink."

"Just because an attractive woman—whose name is Natalie, by the way—wants to come to my place for a drink does not mean she's throwing herself at me."

I grab the tiny green bottle and turn back to him. "Never said she was."

"Your face implied it."

"So, you don't plan on taking her to bed?"

"I probably will end up sleeping with her, yes. But we're adults, living the single life in our early thirties. It's healthy. Based on your judgment, I take it, you haven't had a date in a while."

"I have plenty of men ask me out on the regular."

"I have no doubt that you do. I just never see you

leave here with anyone. Or get dressed up for that matter."

I tap my foot on the floor and bite my lip while I try to think of something witty to say back, but what's the point? I have nothing to hide.

"For your information, I'm just as happy, being here on a deadline, wrapped up in my fictional world for the evening, than being with a man who is a waste of my time."

I push the bottle of limejuice into his chest—a tad bit forcefully—and walk over to the couch, where I was working.

Propping my feet up, I put the laptop back on my thighs and look at the screen. I'm about to start typing again when the cushion next to me dips with the weight of the man taking a seat beside me. When I glance up the bottle is sitting on the counter looking like a forgotten thought.

"What are you working on anyway?" He slings his arm behind me, resting it on the top of the couch.

I roll my head toward him. The scent of his cologne is so damn sexy. I wish he'd bathe in fish oil, so he'd have at least one repulsive trait.

"Don't you have a date next door?"

"She can wait five minutes. You seem like you can use the company. You're awfully on edge."

His eyes curve in concern as he smiles. I know I'm being short with him, which is unfair. I just get so anxious when I start a new book, especially when I have no idea where it's going.

"I'm finishing up a three-book series about brothers. The first hero was a badass racecar driver. The next was this enigmatic CEO, and now, I'm at a total loss. I need him to be bold yet gentle. Sexy yet down-to-earth. He has to be … dreamlike." Yes, even I hear the wistfulness in my tone.

"You do realize, these guys aren't real, right?"

I pop my head over with a scowl. "Better than anything I've ever met in the flesh."

He puts his hand to his heart and acts like he's been shot. "That's cold, Lace."

"I'm sure you're heartbroken."

"You have no idea." The way his eyes glint with a closed-mouth smile makes him seem sweetly endearing. "Maybe I can help. Tell me about what you're writing now."

"Are you sure you have time?"

"You look like you need a hand."

I'm taken aback by his interest in my books. It makes a small grin spread across my face. I sit up straight. "Well, I'm messing around with a scene, just to get a feel for my characters. Tanner—"

"His name is Tanner?"

"It's a romance. I can't name him Fred or Chuck or Barney."

"Why not? Fred's a good name."

"Will you please let me tell you my story? So, Tanner is young because that's been established in the other books. But he can't be a bad boy or a controlling boss because I did that already. I'm thinking something in the creative field."

"Florist?" he asks with a wink.

"It's sweet, and that works for you, but I need something sensual and maybe a little more daring."

His mouth rises on one side as he levels his gaze with mine. "For the record, I'm very daring in the bedroom and incredibly sensual." His words are said in a deep hum.

"Is that opinion or fact?"

"Baby, it's a proven fact." His words are a low, rumbling thunder to my lady bits.

I clear my throat and raise my chin as Jake places a finger to his lips and thinks for a moment.

"What if you make him an artist? Then, you can have him paint her."

"Like on a canvas à la *Titanic* or something?"

"No. He paints her naked body."

My eyes widen as my lips pull to the side. "Well then, that's a new one. I'm impressed you came up with something like that."

He grins. "I can't take all the credit. I have a friend who runs classes for couples, where they do that. Kind of like those wine-and-paint parties you girls do, just less clothing."

He says it so nonchalantly, and I'm sitting here with my jaw on the floor, having no clue this was a thing.

"Have you ever done that?" I'm beyond intrigued.

"Not yet. Would you ever let a guy paint you?" he asks with a slight tilt to his head.

"Hell yeah, I would!"

He coughs, completely taken aback. "Seriously?"

"Why are you so shocked?"

He shakes his head with a smirk on his face. "Because you always seem like a wallflower who hides behind her apartment door."

"That's only because you know me as a neighbor. When it comes to sex, I'm not afraid to experiment." Not that I actually am right now. In fact, it's been five long years, but Jake doesn't need to know that.

He drops his head and lets out a small laugh. "My mind has just been blown a little," he says, turning his sight on me. "Makes me wonder about you."

I blow him off. "Oh, stop. Don't act so surprised. I write romance for a living."

There's a peculiar look in his eyes as they roam over my face. It's a soul-searching stare, the kind that says he's studying me, hoping to find an ending to the story in his mind. I can only hope he's reading me right.

I lean back a little, confused by the intensity in his expression.

"What are you staring at?" I ask.

"You," he says seriously. "You can learn a lot about a woman by watching her when she's talking about sex."

"And what is that?"

His hand rises to my face, and he places the softest of touches to my skin. "Your cheeks are flush, and your shoulders fall back. There's even this gleam in your eyes, like you're about to eat your favorite candy. It excites you, but you're hungry for it. Like you haven't had it in a while."

I swallow. "You can tell that just from looking at me?"

He leans closer, so close that I can feel the heat pouring off his chest and smell the mint on his tongue. His breath tickles my ear as he whispers, "A real man has patience when it comes to women. Not just the ones he wants to bed. He listens. That is what makes a sensual lover."

My heart pounds against my ribs as he settles back, and that grin of his graces his face once again as I rub my thighs.

"You should get back to Natalie," I say.

He blinks at me, as if he almost forgot he had a woman waiting for him in his apartment. "And you have to get back to your pretend boyfriend."

He rises and walks toward the door.

"Have fun, *Tanner*." I wave sarcastically and then point toward the kitchen. "Don't forget your lime juice."

He reaches toward the counter and raises the bottle. "Thanks." When he gets to the door, he opens it and then pauses in the threshold, turning back to me. "Night, Lacey girl."

He leaves, and I let out a heavy breath. My skin prickles, and my pulse is racing. Jake's visit definitely threw me off, and I need to re-center and focus.

I look back down at my computer. That cursor is still blinking, taunting me.

Daring me.

Glancing over at the door, I think of Jake and wonder if he's right.

Maybe my hero should be an artist. Someone patient. Someone who can read body language.

I put my laptop away, pull out my notebook, and start jotting down notes.

Hopefully, my romantic hero will come to life very, very soon.

CHAPTER FOUR

"Lacey Rivers! Oh my God, I am your biggest fan! *The Suit* is my favorite of all your books, although *The Racer* is a close second. I need to know when the next book is coming out."

I smile at the woman standing in front of me with a rolling cart full of books. Peeking down, I can see she has all of my novels with her for me to sign.

"I'm aiming for a January release. I'll announce the date soon," I reply kindly as I take a book from her and start to sign it.

My marker is getting dull, so Charisse, who is acting as my assistant for the day, hands me a new one.

"Thanks."

"The youngest brother is such a mystery. I can't wait to see what you have in store for him," the fan, whose name is Jenny, gushes.

"Me too." I'm smiling as I hand her the book.

She's the twentieth person I've had in line at this

signing at a local bookstore, and it never ceases to amaze me how people take time out of their day to see me, spend their money on my words, and reiterate some of the lines that touched their souls. When one fan showed me a quote from *Fire and Gold* tattooed on her skin, I knew I'd made the correct decision on following my dreams and publishing that first book as an indie release.

With all the books signed, I walk around the table and take a photo with her in front of my banner, the six-foot sign with my name on it. I'm one of twelve authors here today. It's a small signing but a good one. To my left is a mega-famous author, who even I am fangirling pretty hard over. She has so many readers here today that the store owner had to give out tickets to help with crowd control at her line. Someday, that will be me. For now, I'm pretty damn happy with the turnout.

So far today, I've reconnected with six of my closest reader friends in the area, *finally* met a blogger who has been incredibly kind to me, and come face-to-face with the best readers a girl can have.

And they're all dying to know about my next book.

"Does the new book have a title?" another reader asks.

I sway my head from side to side, deciding on if I should wait or let her in on a little secret. "*The Artist*," I lean in and whisper not so softly.

The women in line swoon at the sound of it, and I hush them, asking them to keep mum about it until I make a formal announcement.

Charisse turns to me, surprised. "*The Artist*? I like it. Where did you get that from?"

I sign the next book and hand it to the reader. "My neighbor inspired it."

She curves a brow as we stand up, so we can take a picture together. I do, and then we take our seats again.

"Which neighbor? Wait. The one with the towel who you met when you first moved in?" She snaps her finger as if trying to remember his name. "Jack?"

"Jake," I correct her and greet another reader.

Charisse smiles like the cat that caught the canary. It's distracting.

"Why do you look like you have gas?"

She rolls her eyes. "Because your hot-as-hell neighbor inspired your next title."

"You don't know he's hot."

"Yes, I do. You've mentioned him in the past. The seafoam-green towel—"

"Why is that detail so important to everyone?" I muse. "Never mind. So, yes, he's cute."

"If you're saying cute, then he's hot as fuck," she says loudly and then apologizes to the woman standing at the table, getting her book signed. "Sorry."

"Don't mind me," the woman says. "I've read plenty worse in this one's books. So …" The reader looks down at me and says rather loudly, "Tell us about the hot-as-fuck neighbor."

I widen my eyes to Charisse in a *now, look what you've done* way. "He's a handsome gentleman who just happened to give me an idea. That's all."

Charisse looks at the reader and explains, "I have it on good authority that he has six-pack abs and is a thirst trap."

"You should put him on the cover of one of your

books and bring him to signings," the woman suggests, and I chuckle because that definitely seems like something Jake would do.

We joke and laugh with at least a dozen more readers before the line winds down and the end time to our event draws near.

"That was a great signing!" Charisse says as we're packing up.

"It really was. I can't explain how surreal it was." I unclip my banner and let it roll back into its metal case.

"I remember when you first told me you shelved a book you'd written because you couldn't find an agent to get you a big traditional contract. You were too afraid to self-publish. I wish I could tell that girl what a rock star she was going to be."

"She wouldn't have believed you," I say, sliding the case into a bag.

"She didn't. I tried to tell you that book was incredible. You just had a shit of an ex-boyfriend who made you second-guess yourself."

Her back is to me as she places the leftover books in a box, so she can't see how the mere mention of Michael still leaves a pang. It's a stupid pang that doesn't belong there because he was, as Charisse noted, a shit of an ex-boyfriend.

I ignore the pang, as always, and continue our task, so we can go home.

Because Charisse is the best friend ever, she helps me load my things into a taxi and comes back to my building with me, so I don't have to bring everything inside on my own.

When the car is in front of my place, she takes my rolling cart and a small box from the trunk, and I grab a large cardboard box and walk to the front door. I'm having trouble getting my key in the lock, and I'm startled when a hand comes from behind me and takes the keys from my hand to unlock it.

"Here. Let me get that for you," Jake says as he opens the door wide.

"Thanks." I walk in, and Charisse follows behind me.

I stop near the mailboxes and turn toward her as she walks closer. Her back is to Jake, which is a good thing because her eyes are bug-like as she mouths, *He's hot!*

I roll my eyes at her and start to walk toward the elevator, but Jake moves quickly to me and takes the box out of my hands.

"That's okay. I can carry it," I insist.

He doesn't seem to want to hear it as he grabs the handle of my rolling cart from Charisse's hand and walks in front of us to the elevator.

"Jake, seriously, I'm good."

My words fall on deaf ears because he hits the call button with his elbow, and the doors open. Charisse looks at me with wide eyes and an open mouth, realizing this is the man we were talking about earlier. She rushes into the elevator, almost giddy to talk to Jake.

"Hi. I'm Charisse. The best friend," she says with a huge grin on her face.

Jake nods his head in greeting. "Jake, the neighbor."

Charisse turns to me with an expression on her face that's so smug, like she just found the Christmas stash

37

of toys. We reach our floor and let Jake exit first since he's the one doing the heavy lifting.

While he walks out, she turns to me and whisper-yells, "Now, I am not the *distressed female in need of a hunky hero* type, but a man who takes the initiative to help you carry your shit is a keeper."

"He's not mine," I whisper-yell right back.

"He should be," she says with a shit-eating grin.

I shake my head and push her out of the elevator.

When we finally enter the hallway, Jake is waiting outside my apartment door with a tilt of a smile he's trying to fight on his lips, which makes me think he heard every word from us.

I unlock it quickly and hold it open, so he can come inside and place the box and crate near the table. Charisse puts the smaller box that's still in her hands on the counter.

"Thanks for doing that," I say to Jake as he walks out of my apartment and into the hallway, stopping right outside my door.

"No problem. Just happened to work out perfectly that I ended my evening early and caught you at a good time. What is all this stuff for anyway?"

"Lacey had a book signing, and she was awesome! Sold-out attendance, and everyone was dying to meet our girl."

I flush at Charisse's words.

"Tonight's signing was fun, just a small group of authors at a local bookstore. We each did a reading from one of our books, and then signed for the next two hours."

I'm lucky to have her. She's one of the reasons I have

the life I do. Her encouragement was a huge push for me to hit the Submit button to publish my first book on my own. I wouldn't be living the life I do if it wasn't for her.

"That's awesome." Jake sounds genuinely impressed.

"It was all Charisse. She makes me look much cooler than I am, both at signings and on social media. I like to think of her as my guru." I beam.

"Hell yeah." She high-fives me, and we laugh.

"Do you want to stay for a drink?" I offer to Charisse.

She was kind enough to sit with me today after work. The least I can do is pour a glass of wine.

"Sorry, babe. I have to get home to put Aubrey to bed. She's been giving Melody a horrible time, and she has a deposition to prepare." She turns to Jake and explains, "I have a wife and kid at home. Are you the *wife and kids* type?"

I could kick her for the way she asked that question, like she's ready to play matchmaker for me.

Jake answers her coolly, "Yeah. I would be the perfect husband."

I snort a laugh, wondering if he realizes how cocky he sounds.

Charisse turns to me with that stupid smile still on her face. "Perfect."

"Get out of here, crazy," I say as I hug her. "You were a godsend, like always. Give that baby a kiss for me. I'll call you tomorrow."

She waves to Jake and heads down the hallway. Jake and I are standing here, watching her disappear into the elevator. When she's gone, I turn to him.

"Thanks again for helping me bring that stuff up."

He looks like he's going to say something, but I'm already turning back to my place. If there's one thing that was confirmed today, it's that I need to get my notes straightened out and finalize a plot for *The Artist*.

I'm closing the door when I feel resistance and realize Jake is keeping me from closing it fully.

"Lacey," he says.

I pop the door open.

"Don't forget to have fun." I look at him curiously when he adds, "With your work. If you don't love what you do, it's not worth doing."

I watch as he turns and walks to his apartment. He goes inside, and so do I, walking to my room to change. I grab my notebook to jot down notes. I'm scribbling thoughts down when music pours through the walls.

This time, instead of it being loud and raucous, it's a lyrical love song. The kind you can relax to. Think to.

I smile as I settle into the corner of my sofa and work. Good thing I do love what I do for a living.

That must be why I'm smiling.

CHAPTER FIVE

I'm searching through photos of hot guys reading because, well, there are some perks to writing romance. One of them is getting to fawn over pictures of handsome men. I've actually been Googling away most of the day when there's a knock on the door.

I open it to see Jake standing on the other side, wearing jeans, a navy henley, and that damn smirk. He's dressed casually, yet the way his sleeves are rolled to precise three-quarters makes me think he puts way more effort into his appearance than tossing on a clean shirt.

He looks like he's about to say something when his face falls and his eyebrows turn down in question. "Do you ever wear clothes that aren't sweats?" He points at my attire.

"I was dressed quite nicely for my signing, thank you very much." It might have just been jeans and a sweater, but I did throw on heels, so that counts for something.

"I meant, when you're not greeting your hordes of fans?"

I run my hand over my head, smoothing out any loose strands that might have popped out of my bun. "I'm writing."

"Explain this to me, Miss Rivers. Business hours are flexible, but when do they end?" He steps into my apartment with a white pastry box in his hands and a swagger to his hips.

I close the door, not sure if I'm annoyed because he's here, interrupting me, or if I'm happy for the distraction from the nothingness surrounding me. Plus, whatever is in that box smells heavenly.

"I'm on a deadline, remember? I need to write, so here I am … writing."

"Yes, but that's what you do during the day, not when you should be out, watching the game."

"I don't like sports."

He holds an arm out in the air, as if to stop time and silence my words.

"Don't say that out loud. We're in Bears territory here. And you don't have to like the game to enjoy the two-for-one drinks that are served."

"You have a point, I guess. What's in the box?"

He places it on the counter and unties the string. "The bakery near the shop makes the most amazing treats. The lady who runs it brought these over to me, but there's way too many, so I figured I'd share."

I raise a brow. "That's super sweet of you."

Peering into the box, I see flower-shaped cookies with powdered sugar on top.

"Don't be shy." He pushes the box toward me after grabbing one for himself and taking a bite.

I lean against the counter and grab one. The buttery, sweet flavor melts in my mouth. I let out a moan, making him pause mid-chew, before gobbling up the cookie and licking my fingers of the powdered-sugar residue. My thumb is in my mouth as I gently suck on it , and he looks at me with his mouth agape.

"Why are you staring at me like that?"

He shifts on his feet as he swallows. "Have you eaten today?"

I look up as I try to think if I ate anything. "I had coffee this morning—"

"Get dressed," he commands as he closes the bakery box.

"Why?"

"Because you need to eat and get out of this house of loneliness."

I eye him, wondering what his angle is. We've been friendly since I moved in but more like neighbors saying hi in the hallway, and we hung out for a few minutes the other day when he popped in for limejuice. Other than that, we've never spent more than ten minutes together.

"We"—I motion between the two of us—"don't go out. Where are your girlfriends? What about your lady, Natalie?"

"Who? Oh, the yoga girl. She's a great girl but not for me. Besides, I'm not in the mood to have to romance tonight. I just want to sit back and chill."

"I'm not sure if I should be honored or offended." I walk away from him and head into the living room. I plop down on the couch and grab my computer, which is quickly removed from my lap and in the hands of Jake.

"Have you even stepped outside today?"

"Yes," I lie.

His mouth twists as he eyes my stained sweatshirt. "Yeah, I don't buy it, but I love the way you lie. Come on. Get up."

He hits my leg, nudging me to stand while taking my hand and lifting me up. I stand with my hands on my hips, defiantly looking up at him.

He smiles as if my stance is cute. "We can stay for just one drink and an appetizer, if you're that hung up on staying home and writing. I'm sure your brain needs the break anyway."

Maybe he's right. I've been lounging in the house all day, and writing isn't coming so easily. Maybe a drink will do the trick.

"Fine," I huff and drop my hands from my hips, heading to my room to change. "Where do you want to go?" I call out from behind the half-closed door.

"What do you like? I could have pizza, but I'd prefer something lighter. Gino's is good, but we'd have to wait for a table. Maybe Shooter's? That's the best place, I think. It's on the corner and casual. Sound good?"

I'm buttoning my jeans as I call out, "Sure. I'm not picky."

"Good," he says. "I didn't know you were a Tom Hardy fan."

I roll my eyes as I take my shirt off, realizing he is looking at my computer screen. "It's research. I'm using him as inspiration. Now, there's a real man. Strong and protective, sweet with his wife, loves dogs, and just gets more attractive with age. He's hot, and that accent is totally swoonworthy."

I'm shuffling through my drawers, looking for a shirt, when I hear him say, "I see your research also includes porn. Damn, Lace. You like some kinky shit."

My eyes bug out of my head as I drop the shirt in my hands and storm out of the living room, hopping over the couch and ripping the computer from his arms.

I'm standing here with my chest heaving and the laptop clenched to my stomach when I realize I'm in front of Jake, in my pink lace bra.

His eyes travel from my face to my décolletage and skim over the swell of my breasts, making his chocolate eyes turn black before they pop back up with a smile. "You do know, clothing isn't optional at Shooter's, right? I believe you're required to wear a shirt."

I scrunch my nose at him. "Not funny. And what were you thinking, snooping on my computer?"

"The tab was still up. I must have accidentally clicked on it."

"Accidentally, my ass."

He's making a face like a boy who was caught with a cookie, but I can't prove he put his hand in the jar. I squint at him as I march my shirtless self—and my laptop—back into my room, slamming my door behind me.

As I fall against it, my heart races, and my breasts feel tender beneath my bra. My skin is sensitive, the way it is when I'm turned on. It's weird because nothing happened. All Jake did was run his eyes over my body, but damn, I shiver in a way that's foreign yet familiar.

I focus my energy on getting dressed. With a black

crewneck top and jeans, I head to the bathroom and do my makeup. I might not get dolled up often, but I know how to do a perfect cat eye when necessary. I walk out of my bedroom, and he doesn't seem impressed with my cleaned-up look.

Jake reaches for my bun and the stray hair that's sticking up. "You're not going to do anything with this?"

I glare at him. "You're lucky you're getting me out of the house."

"You look like you put it up in a bun and then had crazy sex. That, or you masturbated." He eyes me playfully. "It's wild and unkempt. I'm totally for the sex-crazed look. I just wanted to know if *you* were okay with it."

My brows lift at his assumption. I mean, he's one hundred percent right that I got myself off while watching porn earlier today, but that's beside the point.

With a slight huff, I turn back to my bedroom, remove my bun, and brush my hair out. It's still bumpy, but it looks presentable.

As I come out, I point at him and declare, "No comments. This is how I'm leaving the house, and that's final. Girls won't think we're on a date, so you'll still get hit on, I'm sure of it."

He grins as he smooths out his shirt. "Not concerned. Now, let's go."

Since Shooter's is nearby, we decide to walk, taking in the warm autumn night. I have to keep up with Jake as he strolls down the street. His long legs move as if he were floating, and I quicken my feet to meet his pace.

We get to the bar, and it's moderately crowded—typical for a Monday night. There are sporting events on the televisions, including a pregame special for the Bears.

Jake grabs a stool at the bar and holds one out for me while calling over to the bartender. He orders a stout for himself and a Manhattan with three cherries for me.

I tilt my head, surprised.

"Manhattans are the superior drink." He grins.

I nod, impressed he remembered.

The bartender places the drinks down. I instantly reach for a cherry, swirling it around in my mouth, tasting the alcohol before popping it off the stem.

"You need to write that in one of your books," Jake says, taking a swig of his beer. "That thing you do with your tongue around that cherry."

"You're such a guy."

"Trust me, it's a good thing."

"Want to see something ridiculous, yet I've heard, it's a huge turn-on?" I don't wait for him to answer as I place the stem back in my mouth and fold it with my tongue. Next, with my mouth closed, I bite on the stem and twist the rest with my tongue until it forms a knot. As I pinch the end and move it from my mouth, I explain to him, "Apparently, if you can tie a cherry stem with your mouth, you're a good kisser."

He nods.

"And blow jobs," I add.

Jake nearly chokes on his beer.

"Sexy?" I ask, thinking the entire thing is silly.

He chuckles under his breath. "Yeah. Definitely write that next time you're showing how the characters develop their attraction for one another. The *hate each other and then fall in love* thing is good, but seduction by cherry stem is straight to the point."

It takes me a few minutes to catch on to what he's talking about. "Wait. Did you read my book I gave you?"

"Of course I did. I can't live next door to a famous author and not read her work."

"You read it?"

"I finished it."

I look down, completely taken aback that he not only opened the book, but he also read it to the end. Here I thought, he was going to use it as a coaster or doorstop.

He leans forward and grabs my attention with his dark eyes, willing me to look at him. "Aren't you going to ask me what I thought?"

I lift a shoulder. "Only if you want to share. Reading is a selective and personal endeavor."

"I loved it."

I look up with slightly narrowed eyes, searching his for any sign that he's bullshitting me. His gaze is steady, and his shoulders are square. His expression doesn't give any clue that he's lying, and all I see is conviction.

"Thanks," I state quietly.

"Your prose was fantastic. I loved how the heroine was feisty yet vulnerable. Her backstory was completely believable, as was the male narrative. I had worried you were going to paint all men as macho Neanderthals who tossed women onto beds and dominated them."

I smile. "Well, I do have a few of those. *Fire and Gold* just happens to have a hero who is sensitive yet can be the protector the heroine needs."

"It was great. And the scene at the end, where the ex-husband comes to take her, how did you know the best place to bury a body?"

Laughing, I cover my mouth with my hand and shake my head. "You can thank Google for that."

Turning on my stool, I take a look around the establishment. It's a modern bar with black leather backed booths and a swanky dance floor with pool tables off to the side. To me, it's exactly the kind of place I would write about, where my hero would take a date if they were coworkers at a firm, coming out for happy hour. I'd have them place a bet on who could go home with someone and get laid first. Of course, they'd leave with one another.

"Is this where you bring your dates?" I ask as I spot a couple chatting ever so closely at the end of the bar.

"No."

"Too close to home?"

"Kind of. I love the food, and the vibe is chill. I come here with friends."

I nod in understanding. "So, where do you take your dates?"

"Cellar Door, Marie-Jeanne, Good Measure—"

"No Alinea or Smyth?" I ask, throwing in the names of Michelin-starred restaurants in our city. What he named were anything but.

He shakes his head. "I like to go to trendy dive bars and cool hangout-type eats." I must look confused, so he turns to me fully, placing his arm behind my chair and explaining, "Say I wanted to impress a girl. If I brought her to Smyth, she'd only like it because it was ritzy and flashy She'd assume I had money and would take her to places like that all the time. I don't want a woman to date me just because of the places I'll take her. Plus, I enjoy hanging out in large groups—double and triple dates. I can't expect my friends to afford the same places I can."

"So, dive bars it is."

"For me, a romantic date is a meal of her favorite type of food and then a movie or a museum. It's not about showing off. It's showing that you listen to what they want."

I tilt my head and take him in—handsome, hardworking, considerate. "You're a good man, Jake Moreau."

He grins in agreement. "I told you I was hero-worthy."

My laughter is a little too loud, and it makes the people around us turn their heads. I take a drink in embarrassment.

"I should be taking notes. I always thought men wanted to put their best foot forward on the first date. You know, flashy car, expensive dinner, trendiest after-hours."

"I love that stuff." He points to his shirt, which must be designer by the way he's using it as an example. "There has to be a balance of what you give and take in a relationship."

"Is this you letting me in on the inner workings of the male brain?"

He laughs deeply. "I'll let the romance novelist into the secret mind of a man, though I might be breaking some kind of male code out there somewhere." He winks, and I let out a sharp laugh.

"Don't worry; your secrets are safe with me." I pause as I let what he said sink in. "Does it worry you that a woman might only want you for your money?" I immediately don't like the way the words came out. Based on his designer clothes and expensive car in the parking lot, I guessed he was well off. "I'm sorry. That was rude. I was assuming—"

"You assumed right. The flower business is lucrative, and the building is paid off, so it's all profit. I keep telling my father he has enough to retire, but working is in his blood. I was raised by an entrepreneur with high morals, who never saw himself as a wealthy man. If I buy fine clothes, I must take care of them. If I invest, I do so in my home. And if I ever marry, I'd do it for life."

"I wish all men thought that way."

"Only the good ones."

I let out a *pfft* sound and take a swig of my drink.

"Man trouble in the past?" he asks.

I groan. "Let's just say, I don't have the best view of the male species."

"I take that as a personal insult."

"You should. Your father might have taught you to marry for life, but you're certainly having fun, mating your way through the dating pool."

"And you have nothing to say about the women who are sleeping around? That's a double standard."

"I'd be hard-pressed to think a woman or two hasn't been led on and perhaps fallen in love with your good looks and charm."

"So, you think I'm good-looking?"

"Hardly the point."

"True, but it's nice to hear. I thought you were immune to me." He winks, and I have to look away, so he doesn't see how the simple act makes me blush.

"I'm immune to men who meander through life like it's their playground. It's a sin."

"You're forgetting who sinned first. Wasn't it a woman who led a man to eat the forbidden fruit in the Garden of Eden?" He acts like bringing up Adam and Eve is the most natural discussion on earth.

I raise my eyebrows in surprise. "So, every time you sin, it's Eve's fault?"

He laughs, and for some reason, the sound makes butterflies flutter in my stomach.

"What I do is not a sin. Sex between two consenting adults is nothing more than using what God gave us. That would be like saying eating is a sin."

I let out a hard laugh. "That is called gluttony."

"Eating too much is a sin. Satisfying the palate is survival."

"Then, you're claiming you need sex to survive?" I give him a deadpan stare.

"Pleasure," he breathes in that low, husky voice. "The human soul needs pleasure or else it will surely die."

I swallow and then take a heaving breath before grabbing my water. I need hydration. "Not buying it." I try to sound unaffected.

He leans back as he wraps his fist around his glass. "Fine. If you can't wax philosophical, then I'll hit you with the facts. Men can get prostate cancer if they don't have a release often."

I rub my lips together, nodding my head and trying not to laugh. "Okay, fine. If science says so, then it has to be correct."

He winks again as he brings the glass to his lips and drinks.

Leaning back in my seat, I bite my lip as I stare at this beguiling man who has an answer for everything and has bested me at my own game of questions. Not only is he handsome, but he's also witty as all hell.

"Can I be honest for a moment?" I don't wait for him to respond as I add, "You're really cool to hang out with."

A dimple appears on his cheek as he grins at my comment. "I knew you'd figure it out sooner or later."

I smile as I finish my cocktail.

The bartender comes back, and we order five appetizers to share—mostly because Jake can't decide on one, so we get all five. We talk for the next two hours. He's funny when he tells me about some of the wild orders he's made at the flower shop, like a John Deere tractor and Elvis Presley for a funeral. He even had a client order a thousand roses for a proposal, only to forget which one he hid the engagement ring in. The man called, furious that the flowers had eaten the ring. Turned out, it was found days later in a shoe.

I tell him about my book signing and the random things fans have asked me to sign. I'll put my pen to anything, but I draw the line at a dildo. That's just not cool.

Our conversation carries us back home as we take the scenic route along the canals, feeling the breeze whipping through the buildings.

When we get to our front doors, I chance a glance at Jake, who is staring at me with a smile.

"Don't look at me like that," he says with a grin.

"And how am I looking at you?"

"Like I drank too much and talked your ear off."

I laugh out loud. "Not you, me! I feel like I didn't shut up all night."

He leans against his door and looks back at me, totally serious. "I could listen to your stories all day."

With a lick of my lips, I look away and roll my eyes. "Night, Jake."

I turn my lock, and before I close it, he calls out to me, "Lace?"

"Yes?" I pop my head out my doorway.

"Break a wrist." He grins as he steps into his apartment.

I laugh at the sentiment. "Thanks."

After I close my door, I stare at my computer, my fingers itching to touch the keyboard. When I do, this time, the words flow in the best possible way.

CHAPTER SIX

"Help me carry the wood into the house," my mother says as I exit my car. She's standing in front of a log splitter, wearing jeans and a T-shirt with her hair pulled back in a low ponytail.

I head over to her pile on the ground, not bothering for our usual hug hello yet since she's in the midst of cutting logs.

"Look at you, all rugged," I muse.

She smiles. "I prefer austere. It has a nice ring to it."

With a giggle, I load the log holder that's sitting on the ground and bring the bag down to the cellar, where she keeps her wood stacked against the wall. There's a decent stockpile down here already, and this new wood will have to dry before she can use it.

When I get back outside, she's grabbing a bunch of logs, loading them into her arms. "I bet I can carry more in my arms than you can in that bag."

I squint my eyes in determination. "You're on."

I put the rest of them in the bag, and together, we bring the remainder to the basement.

Some of my fondest memories from my childhood are doing chores like this. She would somehow always make even the hardest of tasks into a game, so I wouldn't realize just how hard life really was for this *single mother and daughter* duo.

"If you'd waited, I would have helped you split the wood," I tell her.

"A good woman knows how to take care of herself. Besides, this keeps me active and sets my mind at ease." She wipes her hands on her pants and looks up at the sky.

I love seeing my mom with her hands dirty. She has the feminine quality of a dancer with the hardened tone of an independent woman. Her long, thin arms bend as she leans back and stretches, which is graceful in its own way.

"September is late in the year for prepping wood. Where did this come from?" I ask.

"The neighbor had a tree cut down due to rot. He brought this over."

I smile. "That's an awfully heavy piece of tree to be schlepping over here for the nice neighbor lady. Looks to me like Mr. Myers needed a reason to come over."

She narrows her eyes at me. "You know that's not the case." With a point to my outfit, she says, "You look nice. What's the occasion?"

I pull my brown hair to the side as I glance down at my long-sleeved sundress and ballet flats with a shrug. "Just felt like doing my hair and makeup today. I've been living in sweats."

She nods, knowing that's my ensemble of choice when I'm writing. "Come on up. We'll make lunch, and you can tell me about what you're working on."

We go up into the kitchen, which is exactly the same as when I was a child. Floral wallpaper with yellow daffodils and oak cabinets on the wall. It was old and out of date then. It's ancient now.

I take a seat at the eat-in table while Mom gets bread, cold cuts, and mustard from the refrigerator.

That's when I notice the box sitting on the table. It's slightly bent on the top, and it has my name written across the side.

"What's this?"

She smiles big. "Open it. I found it up in the attic. I can't believe I forgot about it."

I open the top, and when I do, memories come rushing back. Every summer, we would go on scavenger hunts, looking for the craziest things we could find and trying to beat the prior year's items.

When I see the Indian arrowhead we found on a hike or the set of oddly shaped magnets we scored at a flea market, my heart fills with joy. We didn't have much, but my mom made sure I had the best upbringing possible.

After I rummage through the box of childhood memories, I push it to the side. "I have an offer from a publishing house."

Her brows rise. "Really? For the romance books?" She sounds more surprised than excited.

"Yes. They're keeping an eye on my next novel. If it does well, then they'll sign me to a three-book deal."

She raises her chin but doesn't smile. "That's very good."

As she takes a seat, I watch her mannerisms, namely the way she keeps her eyes fixed to the bread she's taking out of the bag and the meat she's putting on. Her muscles are stiff, and her mouth is steady.

"You don't approve," I state.

She drops her hands to the table as she looks up. A very small sigh escapes her lips. "Of course I approve. You're a brilliant author. Even when you were six, I could see you had a gift for writing. That's why I've always supported your career choice. I just wish you'd write something with meaning, not this sex fluff. You're better than this."

"It isn't sex fluff. Think of it as women's literature, except when I get to the romance scenes, they're a tad … explicit."

She raises a brow with a smile. "They're a lot explicit. Makes me wonder what you're doing over there, living alone in the big city."

"I'm not dating, if that's what you're asking."

My mom gives me a sorrowful expression. "I know the feeling. Men are destined to stomp our hearts. Take your father for example. That sorry excuse for a man ran off. Good-for-nothing—"

"I got it, Mom. It's not every day you're reminded that your father abandoned you."

Actually, that's a lie. Nearly every time I see my mother, she reminds me that my dad took off. It's been twenty-three years, and she still can't get over it.

It's a shame really. My mother is beautiful with long brown hair and bright blue eyes. Thanks to the manual labor she does around the house, she still has a phenomenal body. But her skin is worn—from sun and a broken heart. The years of being a single mother are written in the wrinkles on her skin. The scar my father left on her heart practically shows through the T-shirt she's wearing.

She's smart too. My mother is a grant writer, the kind who gets schools and philanthropies the funds they need to succeed. I know for a fact that men have been interested in her through the years, but she has carried my father's scarlet letter on her sleeve all this time. She'll never change.

"That reminds me. You have a letter." She walks to the counter and lifts a blue envelope.

I take it from her, looking at the familiar handwriting. "It's not my birthday. Why is Dad sending me a card?"

"Probably because one of your cousins mentioned you'd released a book over the summer. He's an advantageous son of a bitch, that one."

With a grimace, I pop it open and take a look. It's a congratulations card—the kind he should have sent when I graduated high school or college or pretty much every other milestone he missed. The fact that he sent it to my mother's house and not my apartment shows how little he knows about me.

I toss it in the trash and watch my mother.

Her jaw is tight as she looks off to the other side of the room. I hate how Dad makes her feel this way after all these years. Every move she makes is a direct result of him walking out on her.

Charisse's words run through my head. *"Don't turn into your mother."*

NAUGHTY NEIGHBOR

I close my eyes and shake off the idea. "Tell me about work. Any new grants come in?"

Her face lights up. "Actually, yes. I spent hours researching and drafting a large one for that children's museum downtown, and we got it. Thirty-five thousand dollars. Man, seeing the board president's eyes light up when I told her the news was priceless." She smiles proudly, nodding her head. "That's why I keep at it. It's a lot of work for little money and a lot of rejections, but when you get one that's approved, it makes it all worth it."

I sigh wistfully. I know exactly what she means. I get the same satisfaction from writing my books. I just wish she would recognize that. What I do might not fund children's museums, but my books still help people escape from their world for just a bit of happiness.

She hands me my sandwich and we speak about work. As I eat the lunch she prepared for me, I listen to her and realize it's not only the decor or wallpaper that hasn't changed. My mom hasn't either.

As children, we put our parents on a pedestal. We make them out to be these superheroes in our minds. Don't get me wrong; my mom has definitely had her superhero moments, having raised me on her own, but I was about seven years old when I started to see the cracks in her facade.

She would lie and say she was happy my dad had left and that she was stronger because of it, but there were nights I heard her crying. The next day, she'd be here, at this table, talking about work and tasking me to do better with my grades. I realized, the harder she worked, the more she was hurting about something on the inside.

I didn't fully understand it until I was older and had my first heartbreak. His name was Rick. He took my virginity and broke up with me the next day. I sobbed, the sounds coming out of me very similar to the ones I'd heard coming from her door. Just as she held her head high in public, I did too. Poured my heart into taking the SAT and got a near-perfect score.

With the way my mom talks about a new grant she's working on, the kind that is almost unattainable, I know my father's card, now sitting in her trash can, has been bothering her all week. And here she is, cutting wood, making lunch, and changing the world.

I never realized she'd be wearing her mask twenty plus years later. To see her still holding up that facade, being strong and saying she's fine when I can feel it in my bones that she's not, hurts my heart for her.

Yes, I know the issue here.

Hello, kettle. Meet pot.

I'm not turning into my mother. I am already her.

As I leave my mom's house, I feel … *off*. I don't want to say I'm dejected, but as our afternoon together carried on, I found myself noticing way too many similarities about the two of us, like the way she pulls her hair at the nape of her neck when she's concentrating or how she hums when she's cooking. Those little habits are sweet, and I'm proud to be a reflection of her in that way, but the disdain we have toward men and the way we prefer to stay home instead of living life to the fullest have me wondering if I'm going to grow up and be just like my mother—single and alone.

No matter how much I try to deny it, I had fun with Jake last night. It was nice to talk to someone from the opposite sex, to feel that zing you get when someone excites you. It's been years, and I somehow forgot what a night out like that could do for your mental health, if nothing else. I wrote a ton when I got home, and my mind felt freer this morning than it had in years.

Could Charisse really be on to something?

I'm so lost in the thought that I miss my exit and have to take the scenic route home. As I'm driving through the streets of Chicago, I notice Moreau Flowers. The antique lights over the sign are still lit, so before I even realize what I'm doing, I pull over and exit the car. I cross the street and look up at the wooden sign hanging above the storefront. The letters are in script and show the shop has been in business since 1923.

When I open the large wooden door with a glass floral inlay, I see Jake in his slacks and a button-down with a black apron mostly covering his designer clothes. He puts down the long-stemmed roses he brought from the back and talks to a couple at the counter. I stand behind a display as I watch him.

His lips are pursed as he listens to the woman who has her arm wrapped around the man's as she stares up at him with a frown.

"I really had my heart set on all white for our wedding."

The gentleman looks down at her. "Yes, honey, but

three hundred dollars for roses that will die is way out of our budget."

Jake raises a finger as he walks around the counter. "I have an idea. If you want a big centerpiece and you want all white, what do you think of these?" He grabs a handful of hydrangeas from a cooler and walks them back to the centerpiece he's been creating.

Replacing most of the roses with the hydrangeas, he transforms it into a full and lush floral arrangement that is almost prettier than when it was just roses.

"These still give you that pure feeling you want while also staying within your budget. It also has a classic, old-school style, which is what you originally said you wanted," Jake says to the woman and then turns to the guy. "And I can do it for two hundred a piece."

The man's expression softens while the woman bounces on her toes.

"I love it!" She beams.

That debonair smile of Jake's is on full display as he takes down their final order, joking with them and laughing as they shake hands.

As the couple leaves, I step away from the display and give a wave.

He looks up at me with a grin. "You don't have to come in here and hide."

"You knew I was here?"

"I'm a store owner in an inner city. I always know when someone walks in. Plus, you're not that stealthy."

I stick my tongue out at him as I walk up to the wooden counter. Everything in here seems to be original, like it's a piece of Chicago's history.

"To what do I owe this surprise?" he asks.

"Luck, I guess. I made a wrong turn and just happened to see your storefront."

"Lady Luck, huh?" His brows rise as he smiles and walks across the room to a bucket that holds a beautiful pink flower, plucking it from the water and handing it to me. "A peony. They're symbolic of both good luck and good fortune."

I want to roll my eyes at him, but the act is so sweet that I actually grin.

"Jake, can you come help me?" I hear a woman call from the back.

"Coming," he says as he walks through a door behind the counter.

A few moments later, Jake and a woman enter through the same door, both carrying large flower bouquets that are full of vibrant colors of magenta, purples, blues, and yellows.

"These are amazing," I gush at the floral art.

"Thank you." She smiles as she places hers on the counter. "Jake designed them."

I look up at him and his proud stature. "Impressive."

"I hope the client likes them too. They were a big project," he says.

The woman agrees with a nod. "The driver will be here soon to deliver them to the museum. There's a charity ball tonight. I have twenty more in the back."

"Wow. Can I lend a hand?" I ask, which makes her turn to me in surprise at my offer.

"Mother," Jake says, "I'd like for you to meet my neighbor, Lacey."

"It's a pleasure to meet you. I love meeting Jake's friends." She walks around with open arms. "I'm Bobbi."

Even though it startles me, I welcome the embrace from a woman who smells like lavender.

One of her arms is still around me as she turns to Jake. "Is this the girl who lives next door? The romance author?"

He nods his head as I tilt mine to him.

Bobbi looks at me, excited. "I could use your help. We can't get this one to settle down for anything. He has girls come through here all the time, batting their lashes, and not one has piqued his interest."

"I'm holding out for the right woman," he states, and his mother pats his cheek.

"You're thirty years old. Being the coolest guy in the room only holds its luster for so long. It's nice to have a family to come home to, but I'm afraid you'll always be my indecisive Libra." She motions to me as she walks toward the back. "Come, Lacey. You can help us carry these flowers to the front while I tell you about the kind of woman Jake needs."

"Ma, she's not a matchmaker."

"No. She's even better. She's a romantic." Her brows rise as she grins at me for confirmation.

I lift my shoulders as I pass him with a smile.

"For the record, I don't need help with meeting women," he calls as he follows us to the back, acting like a child trying to prove a point.

Bobbi points to the vases she needs moved. "Oh, I'm sure you don't have trouble with getting laid. I'd just like someone to call a daughter-in-law."

My mouth falls at her brazen conversation of sex. I know he's a grown man, but my mother and I would never have such a talk. She said it all fun and casual, as conversations between adults should be.

We're halfway through bringing the flowers up to the front when the driver arrives. Loading everything into the cooler truck is harder than I thought it would be. Jake and Bobbi are constantly making sure every petal is perfect and that the vases are secure in their transport boxes.

While we load, Bobbi tells me all about the type of woman she thinks Jake needs to date. A strong-willed woman who will put up with his antics. A career gal with a big social life of her own, who won't eat up too much of his time because Jake is a social butterfly and the man likes his freedom. Someone from a big family is a bonus because she'll understand how to handle the Moreau clan. And the woman most definitely needs to know how to cook.

As she rattles off her version of the perfect woman, Jake ignores her, tending to the delivery.

The truck drives away, and we head back inside. Bobbi goes to the back, and Jake and I are left in the front of the shop.

"Your mom is great," I say with a grin.

"She's a spitfire; that's for sure." His tone oozes sarcasm.

"She's also very beautiful. You look just like her. The eyes are captivating."

He smiles. "My eyes *are* quite nice."

I hit him in the arm. "I meant, your mom's. Man, you're vain."

He rubs his arm as he laughs. "No, you specifically

gave away that you check me out. What other things do you notice about me?"

I start to walk away, but he grabs my arm.

"I'm only teasing." He twirls me back to face him, and I glance at his handsome face. "Besides, I notice things about you too. Like how pretty you look in this dress."

I bite my lip and turn away. "Thanks."

He places his knuckle to my chin and brings my gaze back to him. "Don't get bashful like that. You're a gorgeous girl when you stop hiding behind those big sweats. Your hair looks nice too."

"Are you implying I need makeup and nice clothes to be pretty?"

He doesn't smile, nor does he flinch. "I'm saying, you should show off your beauty more often. It's striking."

I inhale a deep breath and take in the magnitude of his compliment. I'm often complimented on my wit and prowess but never my looks. I've always found pride in the fact that my mind is my best feature. But if I'm being honest, hearing these words from this man makes my stomach flutter.

"Now, forgive me if I'm wrong, but I think you came here for a reason."

His words have me staring up at him, confused.

"And what do you think that is?"

"I don't know, but I might have just the cure for whatever is bugging that little head of yours." He takes his apron off and places it behind the counter. "You remember my friend I told you about who owns that art studio? There's a class tonight, and I can get us in."

NAUGHTY NEIGHBOR

My thoughts go blank for a moment before revving back up and processing what he said. "You want us to paint each other?"

"Yeah. It would be great research for your book, and if you like it, you can write about it."

With a deep exhale, I take a step back. "I don't know. That seems so intimate."

"I don't mind." He sounds so casual. "It could be fun, and I promise to be a gentleman. It's a public class, so it's not like we'll be naked or anything."

I sway my head from side to side as I take in his proposal. I've never, ever done something like this. Hanging out with a risk-taker like Jake could be good for my writer's soul. Plus, I'm desperate for more of the writing mojo he gave me last night.

I toss my hands up in the air and declare, "Sure, let's do it. Experiencing it will totally help me write it more clearly. Okay, I'm in."

Jake's face lights up as he checks his watch. "The class is at eight, so if you hang out a bit while I lock up, we can drive there together."

He heads to the front and locks the door before starting his closing procedure. I take my time in walking around, checking out each flower and breathing in the beauty that nature provides.

When I turn around to ask Jake about a certain flower, I catch him staring at me. He doesn't try to hide it either. The way his eyes are intensely on mine makes me redden, and I quickly turn away, not sure how to handle the feeling it causes inside me.

CHAPTER SEVEN

The art studio is located on the second floor of a warehouse on the industrial side of town. It's a loft with giant black-paned windows, which are covered with a sheer material to keep the sunlight in but the onlookers out. Metal beams run along the ceiling, and the floor is concrete with varying shades of gray.

"Jake Moreau!" A guy with a long beard, wearing jeans with paint smeared all over, walks up to us, and the two slap hands. "I was surprised when you said you could make it."

"It was a spontaneous decision. That, and I had to find the right partner." Jake lays a hand on the small of my back. "Rex, meet Lacey."

"Pleasure to meet you," I say, shaking his paint-coated hand. "Not much privacy though, huh?"

Rex lets out a barking laugh. "Don't worry. This is as conservative or risqué as you'd like to make it. We request no nudity though. Keep all the bits covered up."

I'm relieved at his words and also kind of intrigued. Having someone paint me totally naked sounds amazingly sexy.

"I bet you make a killing here around Valentine's Day," I say.

Rex thumbs over at Jake. "I keep telling this guy we need to work together. Flowers and painting obviously go hand in hand."

"Nah. My father is old school. He likes to keep the shop running the way my grandparents did and their parents before them." Jake puts the attention back on me, moving his hands to my shoulders and giving them a rub. Maybe I'm super stressed, but it feels really, *really* good. "Now, where this fits even better is in Lacey's books. I'm hoping she might get some inspiration. I'm just here for the ride to help this one."

"I'm certain this place will inspire you. Follow me. We'll get you guys set up."

Rex leads us through the room of about ten couples, each spread out throughout the loft. We stop at a table in the corner with a tarp on the ground in front of it and two plastic folding chairs facing each other.

"So, who's getting painted on, and who's doing the painting?"

Jake sticks his hands in his pockets and rocks on his heels.

I back away from the tarp and say, "I need to be able to focus for the research."

"Yeah, but don't you also need to know what it feels like to be painted? Like, from the girl's point of view?" Jake suggests.

Rex laughs, ushering us to take our seats. "Choice is yours, but a lot of our couples like to paint each other. You can paint the whole body or just a portion. The rules are … there are no rules."

A devilish grin crosses Jake's full lips. "I like the sound of that. You game, Lace?"

Am I game enough to let this man paint my skin? "Fine, but I get to paint you first."

Rex leaves and comes right back with a tray containing paint bottles, brushes, and a palette for the paint.

"Deal," Jake says, and I feel like I'm making a much bigger deal than just who gets to paint whom first.

"Here is everything you need. You can use brushes or your hands. Totally optional. And you have all the paint you'll need," Rex points to the items on the tray. "We ask that you pour the paint out in small doses, so it doesn't get wasted. Tonight's lesson will be flowers, just for you." He hits Jake's arm.

"Because I don't see enough of them every day?" Jake laughs.

"No, because I figured you know them enough that you won't have to think of what they look like. Envisioning what you want to draw can be the hardest part for some people."

"Thanks for the vote of confidence," Jake says, taking off his jacket.

Rex smiles at me before he goes to greet the next couple who just arrived.

I place my purse down on the far side of the folding table and take in all the tools and colors I have to paint with. Couples around us are talking to one another, some laughing and others in intimate whispers. Between the space and the scene laid out before me, my mind is rushing with words and ideas for a chapter, and I haven't even touched anything yet.

That is, of course, before I turn around.

And see Jake.

Shirtless.

It's no lie. I've always found him attractive, and his face is just the tip of the hot-man iceberg. A well-defined, chiseled chest with a smattering of hair leads down to six-pack abs, which I've written about many times yet never touched in the flesh. His arms are strong with each muscle outlined to perfection.

Tall, big, handsome, athletic, broad, powerful … I need to up my adjectives when I describe a man.

There is definitely a reason I remembered that seafoam-green towel.

Our eyes meet, and it's obvious he knows the sight of him just caught me off guard for all the wrong reasons, so I grab a bottle and pour paint onto my plate.

Rex begins the class by instructing us to coat our partners with a base color. When deciding on which color to choose, I take my time to really look at Jake. I see the way his eyes are brown, but they have a dark circle that lines them entirely. His jaw is straight, and his right eyebrow has a scar that runs through the length of it. He's definitely not Tom Hardy, yet he'd be a damn good hero to explain in every detail.

I reach for the green paint for the base color. I dip the paintbrush, coating it on both sides to get the most coverage before sliding my stool closer to him.

"I'm letting you paint me first, but I have one rule."

He points his finger at me. "Nothing on my sides."

Smashing my lips together, I try to hold back my laughter. "Are you ticklish?"

His brow quirks and I can tell he doesn't want to admit it. He points at me instead. "No sides. Deal?"

Lifting my brush, I hold it up for him to see. "Okay, ticklish man, you got a deal. I won't paint your very delicate skin."

"Trust me, there is nothing delicate about me."

He raises his chin slightly as he sits taller and opens his arms just a little bit, giving me full access to his chest.

As I make the first stroke on his body, I feel his breath hitch before he takes a deeper inhale. I move the brush down his pecs and back up, surrounding the area with a magnificent, rich green that complements his skin tone perfectly.

Once the base is finished, Rex instructs us to choose what flower we have in mind, and I instantly think of the peony he gave me earlier. As I swirl red and white together to get the pink I'm looking for, I keep glancing over at Jake, who never takes his eyes off of mine.

"Your mom seems pretty adamant about marrying you off." I try to use conversation as a distraction.

"She certainly has her mind set as to what I need." It's easy to sense the morose tone in his voice.

"So, a strong-willed woman isn't your type?" I lift the paintbrush and make a small stroke right over his pectoral.

His chest rises with the touch. I'm leaning forward, making the petals, using the folding table to keep my balance. It's a little awkward.

"I don't want a shrinking violet," he says, taking my

73

hand that's wrapped around the edge of the table and placing it on his thigh. It's hard beneath my palm. I blink as my hand flexes over the chiseled muscle and look up at him. "But I don't mind a woman who is willing to learn from me. With me."

The warmth he radiates sends chills to places I should not be feeling right now. I have to close my eyes for a brief second, so I can gather my wits.

I scoot closer while trying to steady my breathing. "That doesn't sound so bad. What other attributes would you want in a woman?"

My hand brushes against his skin again, and the smoothness that encases his toned abs makes me want to lick my lips. I take a deep inhale and glance up at him. When I notice he's staring at me, my heart pounds even more.

I had no idea this would be so intense.

"I like the give and take of a relationship. Someone who complements me but also challenges me. I value a woman who is well put together." His eyes skim over my perfectly lined eyes. "Sophisticated, bright, socially curious." His brows rise, and I laugh lightly. "Fair-minded, an excellent conversationalist, and above all else"—he pauses, and I still my brush, waiting for his words—"honest. That…is what I want."

Here I am, in a room full of people I don't know, yet if I close my eyes, I feel like I'm only with him.

Seeing him.

Feeling him.

The way his breath tickles my neck. The way I can smell his cologne even though the scent has faded some, making it obvious he put it on hours ago. His manly scent comes through the added one, and it only reminds me of the times I lay with a man, woke up with him by my side, and felt comfortable, wrapped in his arms.

It's been too long …

I want so badly to drop the brush and paint with my hands. I'm dying to feel his skin under my fingertips, not just by the side of my hand resting against him.

I swallow as I sit back, getting green paint on my brush. I swirl the tip of the brush down the ridges of his stomach. His body jolts when I get too close to the side.

"Sorry, I tried to tell you I was ticklish," he says.

I grin before moving back in and finishing the flower. Before I make my final stroke, he places his finger on the side of my face, tucking a stray hair that fell. The simple gesture feels familiar.

"I like seeing your face as you paint."

I clear my throat and sit back. "I'm finished. What do you think?"

He looks down at his chest and gives a smirk in approval. "You did good. I'm impressed." He raises his eyebrows at me. "My turn."

I lean down to meet the end of my dress, moving it up my body.

He stops me before I pull it up too far. "Are you sure you're okay with taking off your clothes? I mean, I can paint your arm or even your hand."

I've always been modest, but something about being with him gives me a touch of brazenness and has me brushing his hand away.

I'm only wearing a dress, so I have to lift it and remove the entire thing, leaving me in a pair of black lace panties and a matching demi cup bra. "Where do you want to start?"

I see the hesitation in his expression as he swallows, his Adam's apple bobbing with the action. His fists clench on his thighs while his chest expands with sharp, heavy breaths. "Lace on Lace."

I giggle nervously. "It's like wearing a bathing suit. Except it's my underwear in a room full of strangers. I'm banking on the fact that they're all too infatuated with each other right now to notice."

"They're infatuated all right."

I hold my arms out to him. "I am your canvas."

He takes a brush and studies me with a furrowed brow. "Where would you like me to paint?"

"Anywhere you'd like."

A slow, sexy smile crosses his lips as he dips the brush in a ruby red.

"Now, it's my turn to ask the questions," he says as he paints. Starting at my clavicle, he makes thin strokes, cascading down toward the swell of my breasts and stopping short of the lacy fabric. "Why don't I ever see you leaving the building on a date?"

Tingling sensations run from my chest down to my core as the brush lines the skin.

"I'm happier with the men I conjure up in my head than the ones in the real world."

"Are you sure?"

Every time he lifts the brush to get more paint, I feel myself taking a desperately needed breath.

"I don't know who he is, but the man who caused you to escape into your world of fake heroes and hide from the touch of a man was a coward."

With him so near, I have a hard time breathing. He gets closer to give more detail to one of the rose petals he's painting, and as I feel his breath against my skin, goose bumps instantly cover my body.

"How so?" I pant lightly.

His head is close to mine, and he only turns to meet my eyes. "He was too afraid that he wouldn't be able to handle a gorgeous, fiery woman."

Seeing him stare at me from such a low position causes a sharpness in my chest. I stumble over my words as I take a shaky breath in. I'm finally able to whisper, "I bet you say that to all the girls."

He grins, and chills cover me again. "Only when I absolutely mean it."

The peony I drew on his chest pales in comparison to the bold, large petals of the flower he's making on me. Mine is puny while his is majestic.

"You're an artist," I say, catching him off guard. "The florals you create at the shop is an underappreciated art form. I'm in awe of you."

"Says the woman who weaves words to make romantic heroes that women only dream about."

"So, you agree they don't really exist," I challenge.

"Maybe you just need to dream while you're awake."

His words are poignant. I always feel like I'm dreaming when I'm writing, mixing prose together to create a world that only exists under the veil of night and literature. I don't only want to feel these emotions when I'm reading a book. I want to touch and experience it in the light of day.

Swiping my finger in black paint, I slowly lower my hand to his golden skin and run it over his chest, feeling the heated skin and then flexing my hand over it. His heart beats wildly beneath my palm as I smear it down his body, running over every bump of his abs.

His gaze lifts to mine as his lips part. Placing his brush on the table, he follows suit, swirling his fingers in lavender and then laying them on my ribs. He lets his hand dance from left to right across my body, making me suck in air at the heady sensations that settle low, just at the top of my panties.

With blue, I explore his arms, and with pink, he caresses mine.

When my hands move to his sides, he laughs but doesn't pull away, just as I let him coat my throat before his finger travels down my spine and settles near my ass.

This is, without a doubt, the sexiest thing I've ever done, and we're hardly touching each other in a titillating manner. Having Jake's hands on me is such a damn turn-on that I feel like we've had an hour of foreplay.

Our breaths are heavy, and our laughter is deep, depending on what we're doing to the other. It all feels so good, and I don't want it to end.

Rex walks over to check on us. "You two are pros at this. You both look great. What did you think?"

Besides the fact that I'm totally and utterly turned on right now?

"Very cool spot, Rex. I'll be sure to check it out again," Jake says nonchalantly, like he's not affected the way I am.

I hate that I feel a pang of disappointment at the thought of him coming here again with someone else.

They both turn to me.

"What did you think, Lace? Glad you came?" Rex asks.

"This is most definitely a place I'll never forget."

"Nice," Rex says with a huge smile. "Let's get you home while the image is still fresh in your mind, and feel free to plug my shop name in the book." He winks.

For a moment, I forgot the reason we came. While I loved being part of the scene, I have to remind myself that I'm only here for research.

Jake stands, and I laugh at the mess I made of his chiseled body.

I lean forward and touch his hand. "Thank you."

"For what?"

"Being so supportive." I raise a shoulder and try to explain, "When I went to your shop, I needed a distraction. My mom isn't so keen on what I write, so it's good for my heart to know that I have a friend who thinks it's cool enough to help me get through my writer's block."

That grin that I've come to adore graces his face.

"You know, you can totally pay me back by going home, wearing only your underwear the entire drive."

I laugh at his joke, and yet my mind is reeling. The words to a new scene are fresh in my head, and my literary hero is more real than I ever imagined.

CHAPTER EIGHT

"Oh, this would look so cute on you," Charisse says as she holds up a dress.

She asked me to join her on her lunch break to run to her favorite boutique that's having a flash sale.

She's right; it is nice, but I can't think of an occasion where I'd actually wear it. It's a glittery-gold shift dress with long sleeves, a low neckline, and short hemline.

"It's very pretty, but I like casual slip-on dresses that can be dressed up or down, depending on what kind of shoes I slide on with it. *This* is definitely something you'd wear on a hot date … with a billionaire sexual dominant."

She gives me a deadpan stare. "That's where your mind goes?"

I laugh as I hold it up to her. "You and Melody could go out for a night on the town. I'll watch Aubrey."

"Nope, this is what a single girl in her twenties wears on a first date. You're trying it on."

Clarince takes the dress and spins me toward the mirror on the wall, holding the hanger to my neck to showcase how the dress would look on me.

The way the colors mix with the material brings out my skin tone. And I like how the flecks of gold dance under the store lighting.

When my eyes meet hers in the glass, she scrunches her nose at me. "You're totally digging it."

"Fine, I'll try it on but no promises."

We walk the clothes in our arms—the gold dress for me and a navy one for her—to the dressing rooms in the back, each taking a stall and placing the hanger on the knob on the wall.

I'm slipping out of my yoga pants as she calls over, "How many words did you get in? Are you making the end-of-the-week deadline that Wendy gave you?"

While I'm nowhere near ready to submit a story to my agent, I am feeling better. Last night, I came home and wrote the most intense love scene, where my hero laid the heroine down on a white sheet, painted her naked body from head to toe like she was a living canvas, and then ravaged her with passion. It was hot, sweet, angsty, and damn … it left me turned the hell on.

I might not know how my characters got to that moment, but at least now, I know where they need to get to.

"Oh yeah, I forgot to tell you! Remember how my neighbor, Jake, suggested making Tanner an artist? One of his friends runs this place where couples paint each other, and he took me there last night, so I could experience it firsthand. I finally have my character, and it all makes sense that he was such an enigma because he's a moody artist."

When she doesn't respond, I pause and listen to see if she's still in the dressing stall next to me.

"You okay in there?" I ask.

There's some slight ruffling, and then the curtain to my dressing room is pushed open, making me cover my near-naked body with the gold dress. Charisse, on the other hand, is standing there like a madwoman in the navy-blue dress with a stunned expression and her mouth agape.

"You went body-painting with Jake?" she exclaims with wide eyes. "And you're just telling me this now?"

I roll my eyes and go back to taking my dress off the hanger. "It was no big deal. His friend owns the place."

"Yeah, but did he actually paint you?"

I try to fight the grin that instantly comes back from the memory because I know she'll read more into it than it was. Shoot, even I started to read more into it, but how we stand was made very clear in the way he said good-bye at his door, like we had just happened to enter the building at the same time and didn't just have our hands all over each other.

I close the curtain with a huff. "Yes, I let him paint me but only after I painted him."

"And …" she says, her voice rising in anticipation.

"And what?" I step into the gold dress and slide my arms through the sleeves. "It was fun. You and Melody should definitely try it. I'll watch Aubrey for you."

"Because that's a place where couples go."

I slide the curtain open and give her my back to zip

me up. "No, it's where people of all relationships go to experience something new."

When I turn toward her, she gives me her back, so I can zip her. "Great. You and I can go then."

"I'm not painting you."

With her dress fastened, she spins around with a grin. "Thank you for proving my point. So, is there something going on between you two?" Her shoulders shimmy back and forth as the grin grows on her face.

"You know nothing's going on between Jake and me. That's like Neighboring 101. The dos and don'ts of living next to each other. He was just helping since he knew I was stuck."

"Okay, well, that's actually good because we told Tommy you wanted to go on a date with him."

Now, it's my turn to look like a madwoman. "Charisse! You didn't!"

She grabs my shoulders and pushes me toward the large three-paned mirror at the end of the room, where we can see our outfits from all angles.

"Come on, Lacey. He's super cute, and I think you two will totally hit it off. Plus, you need somewhere to go in this hot little number."

The dress clings to me like a second skin. I like how the sleeves are long, giving the attention to the plunging neckline. The hem is short but not quite as short as it seemed on the hanger. It falls mid-thigh, which actually makes my legs look long and lean.

"I do like the dress, but I'm not going on a blind date."

With her hands on my shoulders, she gives me a

knowing expression. "Your body deserves to go out in this dress. Your feet deserve to wear those Christian Louboutins you bought last year and have only worn once. And your heart really, really deserves for you to get out and laugh with a handsome man over drinks and witty conversation."

I hate the look she's giving me. It's the kind a concerned mother gives her daughter. I know she makes a solid point. The dress is cute, and I *do* love those shoes. And if I'm being totally honest with myself, it was nice to have Jake's hands on me last night. Maybe I am ready to get back out in the dating world and meet Tommy the accountant.

Of course, there's always the chance he could up and leave and break my heart.

"Stop thinking about how the relationship can go wrong before you even go on a date with the guy."

My best friend really does know me too well.

"What kind of romance writer are you if you won't give romance a chance for yourself?"

I waver for a bit before throwing in the towel. "Fine. Give him my number." I sigh. "But I'm only promising one date."

"Good, because Melody already texted him, and he'll be calling you tonight."

She runs toward her dressing stall, and I laugh, chasing after her.

NAUGHTY NEIGHBOR

Tommy called last night, and he actually didn't sound too bad. He was polite, made some jokes about being set up on a blind date, and even asked me where I would like to go. My jittery nerves are at bay as I get ready now for our date.

I slip on my new gold dress and pull my hair half up with big curls in the back. After applying mascara, some neutral eye shadow, and rouge to my cheeks, I glide on a light gloss and take one last glance in the mirror as I hear a knock on my door.

He's a few minutes early, so I hop as I try to walk to the front, putting on a shoe at the same time.

"One sec!"

When I open the door, I'm taken aback when I see the man standing in the hallway.

Jake is here, looking handsome in slacks and a button-down, his hands behind his back. His blond hair is styled back to perfection, making his masculine features even more pronounced. While he appears just as gorgeous as always, it's the slight tilt of his mouth and the lustful gaze in his eyes that catch me off guard.

"Wow," he breathes. "I was just coming over to see if you had any cherries, but damn, you look—"

"Too much? Like I'm trying too hard? A prostitute from a bad '90s movie?"

"Hot." The word is said like no truer word has ever been spoken.

I grin shyly. "Oh. Well, thank you."

"Where are you going?" He steps into my apartment, and I close the door behind him and take a seat at my table to fasten my shoe.

"I have a date," I say, fixing the buckle.

When I look back up, I notice the bouquet of purple flowers he must have had behind his back as he drops the flowers to his side.

"You. Have a date?" His voice does nothing to hide his shock.

"Yes. Don't sound so surprised. Nice flowers, by the way."

He sets them on my counter. "We had a shipment of lilacs come in, and I thought you'd like them."

I rise from my seat and pick up the bouquet. "You brought these for me? Really? That's so sweet of you." Leaning forward, I inhale their scent and close my eyes. "You are so lucky you get to work with fresh flowers all day. It must be euphoric."

With the bouquet in my hands, I walk past him and into the kitchen to grab a vase.

He turns around and follows me. "Yeah, it's nice. Now, back to your date. Who is he?"

"My friends, Charisse and Melody—you remember Charisse. You met the day of my signing. They set it up."

"A blind date?" He sounds relieved. "That makes sense."

"How so?"

"We've already established you don't date."

"Well, there's a first time for everything."

I'm opening the bouquet while simultaneously filling the vase up with water when Jake takes the space next to me.

"Wait. You should only use room temperature water. The stems are very delicate. Do you have cutting shears?"

With a furrowed brow, I search around the kitchen

and find my scissors from the knife block. "Will these work?"

He grins. "They'll do just fine."

I watch as he unwraps the cellophane and tissue paper and puts them in the trash before cutting the rubber band holding the stems together. He moves the now-filled vase to the counter but leaves the water running.

"The trick is to cut the stems at a forty-five-degree angle to increase the surface area of the water intake." He delicately holds each stem under the water and carefully cuts. "Cutting under the faucet helps prevent air bubbles that block the stem from taking in the water. Add one of the flower packets to the water."

I do as he said and watch as the white substance dissolves. "This seems like an awful lot of work for something that is going to eventually die."

"Even though you know they won't last, it's important to enjoy them for as long as possible."

I let out a light laugh. "Sounds like most of my relationships."

He's not laughing back. "You're just in the wrong ones."

The intense smolder in his stare makes my breath hitch. I'm trying to think of something witty to reply with, but the knock at the door gets my attention.

Once I get to the door, I grab the handle, stopping to take a breath before opening it.

"You must be Lacey." A man with a buzz cut and hazel eyes holds up a small bouquet of flowers.

"And you must be Tommy." I take the flowers from him and usher him inside. "Come in."

He enters my apartment and stops short when he sees Jake putting flowers in the vase. Compared to the vibrant lilacs, his bouquet of closed-bud roses look sad.

"Oh. Hello," Tommy says.

"Sorry, this is my—"

"Hi, I'm Jake, Lacey's friend. I live next door." Jake walks over with an outstretched hand and a big smile, putting Tommy at ease. "You got our girl roses. That's great. Here, let me take those."

I hand my bouquet to Jake and watch as he starts unwrapping them from the package.

"He's a florist," I explain to my date, who seems confused by the man in my kitchen.

"That's cool," Tommy says, placing his hands in his pockets. "I don't know a thing about flowers. The ladies at the store helped me pick those out. It's not often you find a guy in one of those places."

Jake's smile grows even wider. "They certainly made sure you didn't overspend. You don't know how often I get guys in my flower shop who want to buy the long-stemmed roses to impress a girl, but then most decide they don't want to spend that much even though the quality is superior than you'll find elsewhere. So, they go to the corner store and get ones like these"—he looks at the bouquet as if the short-stemmed roses offended him—"which won't last long. But you get what you pay for, right?"

I squint my eyes at Jake and tell him to cut the act and then look to Tommy, who doesn't seem thrilled by Jake's presence or his rhetoric.

"I think they're beautiful and very sweet." I smile at Tommy. "Thank you. Shall we go?"

"Sure," Tommy turns away from Jake. "I hope you like the restaurant I chose."

"I'm sure it'll be great. I don't get out much." I reach for my purse.

He takes in my ensemble, eyeing me up and down, and lets out a whistle. "You should. You look amazing. Charisse played down your beauty for sure."

Jake starts coughing, and we turn to see him putting his bouquet of lilacs in the center of my table.

"Lock the door before you leave?" I ask him as we step out of the apartment.

Jake walks us out and waves from my doorway. "You two have a great night. And don't eat Brussels sprouts. They make you gassy. But get crazy with the garlic. It makes everything taste better."

I ignore Jake as Tommy and I get in the elevator. I watch as the doors close on his proud-dad stance in the middle of the hallway, waving like he's sending his kid off to prom.

We make our way to Tommy's car, where he opens my door for me. I know it's been years since I've been on a first date, but I don't even think Michael ever did that for me. It makes me wonder if I've ever had one of my heroes open a door for his girl. I definitely should.

I sit in the passenger seat and see he has a garter belt hanging from his rearview mirror. I squint my eyes as I take in the white lace with a blue ribbon strung through it.

Tommy gets in the car, and when he starts it, music blasts the new Lady Gaga song through the speakers. To my surprise, he doesn't turn it down. Instead, he nods at me with a grin as he backs out of the parking space and drives.

When we pull up to the restaurant, he puts the car in park and doesn't say a word. He exits the car and jogs around to open my door. He puts his hand on the small of my back and leads me inside. The gesture should be simple, but his hand on my back is like a heavy weight. Instead of it feeling natural, it's like I can't do anything but want to cringe with his hand on me.

When we get inside, I step away from him.

"Okay then," I hear him whisper under his breath.

The hostess greets us. "Reservations?"

"Yes, under Thomas Cosgrove. I reserved the corner booth."

"Actually …" I interrupt the two of them and point toward the upscale bar area. It has cool blue mood lighting and a hip vibe. Plus, it's not the *corner booth*. "Can we order from the bar?"

"Of course. I'll set you up in there."

The waitress leads us toward a high-top in the bar area. It's not the actual bar, but it's still a private table with high-back leather stools and ambient lighting. She hands us menus and says a waiter will be by shortly to take our drink order.

"So," I start while he looks at the menu, "Melody says you're an accountant."

"Yes. I work for corporate accounts. When I was in college, there was a major hiring freeze in the country, so I did a search on the best jobs to get hired in, and *voilà*, I found my career. Everybody needs an accountant. Businesses, nonprofits, schools … you and me. It's stable work, so don't worry; I won't be asking you to pay for dinner or front me rent money."

I laugh at his joke because it's the polite thing to do.

"Melody said you're self-employed. I know it's not something you discuss on a first date, but I'd be happy to look at your books and help you find ways to save money. Like, tonight for example. I'll be writing it off as a business expense."

I lift a brow. "Because we're talking taxes, I'm a business meeting?"

He lifts his water glass. "See? Money saved. Order whatever you'd like."

"You must also be very time efficient during tax season."

He grins. "I'm in corporate, so it's always the busy season. When I'm with someone, I like to get in and get out."

I want to laugh at how horrible that sounds for his bedroom antics, but I hold back my bad joke.

"What do you do for a living? Melody wouldn't say. She thought it would make great first-date chatter."

"I write romance."

He laughs loudly. "Really?"

"Yes, really. Why do you think that's funny?"

"Romance? You mean, like those books that have Fabio on the cover?" With his chest puffed out, he pushes his arms back and poses like you'd see a male model doing on the cover of a tawdry historical romance.

"Um, no. Not that there's anything wrong with those. I've actually read quite a few and enjoyed them. But I write contemporary romance."

"There's a difference?"

I pause and think. "Well, it's romantic literature that primarily focuses on the developing romance and relationship between two people. Being contemporary means the book takes place in the here and now, so my characters are experiencing difficulties that you and I would on a daily basis."

"Like what?" he asks, leaning on the table with his arms crossed.

"Navigating the online dating world, wanting to have a baby when you're single and in your mid-thirties, falling for your boss—"

"Going to sex dungeons." His eyes widen with excitement, which creeps me out.

"Going on horrible first dates." I raise my eyebrows at him, silently telling him to get his mind out of the gutter.

Tommy leans back and apologizes, "Sorry. I thought that was part of your genre."

I explain, "It is. And I've read countless dirty books that I love. But those are erotic. My books are sweet yet steamy when you get to the love scenes. I like to explore the relationship deeper, watch my characters grow, and—" My eyes meet his, and I stop suddenly. "Sorry. This is totally inside baseball. It's like if you started talking to me about amortization."

"I really could." He grins, and I shake my head with a fake laugh, knowing the word *amortization* is about as far as my interest in the subject goes.

"So, what else do you do?" he asks with an unsure inhale.

"In terms of …"

"For work."

I give him the side-eye. "That is my job."

"You're a self-employed writer?" He seems disturbed by this info.

I nod with my eyebrows raised. "Yes. I make a good living actually."

"Interesting," he says in a dismissive way as he turns his attention back to his menu.

I place my hands on the table before I announce, "I have to use the ladies' room. If you'll excuse me."

He stands when I do, which is very courteous, so I try to bring down the irritation brewing inside of me. "Sure. Should I order you anything?"

"Yes. Please order me a Manhattan."

"Isn't that a manly drink?" He scrunches his face like women should only drink lemon drops or white wine.

"I don't know. Are you going to order one too?" I tilt my head, daring him.

"Nah, I'm ordering a beer."

"Well then, in this case, the beer would be the manly drink." I tap the table with my hand twice, my point made clearly.

He quickly raises his eyebrows in response as he lets out a breath. I turn and head toward the restroom, taking a long time because I need a break.

Something about this date is not going as planned.

"Nope. Lacey, you will not sabotage this date before it's even begun. He was just asking questions. You're navigating the first-date crash course. You'll find your stride. Give it to the end of dinner."

Thankfully, there's no one in the restroom to hear me give myself a pep talk.

I freshen up my lip-gloss and check my dress again. Feeling renewed, I walk out of the restroom to see my table is empty.

First, I assume he went to the men's room until I notice him at the bar, talking to a woman in a rather intimate way. When I see them exchange numbers, I shake my head, knowing my instincts were right. Instead of giving him another second of my time, I walk straight for the door, opting to take a bus home rather than stay for dinner.

CHAPTER NINE

"Would you like more wine?" I ask Charisse as I hold up the bottle.

She picks up her glass. "How dare you even ask. Of course I would. Melody's driving tonight. And she's putting Aubrey to bed when we get home." She turns to give Melody a huge smile, and I know that wasn't originally part of the plan.

Melody laughs as she picks her daughter up off the floor. "I guess I should have known that would be the deal."

"It's the least we can do since we set my best friend up with a douche in a suit." Charisse gives me a sorrowful expression as she takes a sip.

"Tommy is a nice guy," Melody explains for the thousandth time. "How he behaves in the office and on a date are two very different things. I'm sorry he hit on someone else."

Waving my arm in the air to push away the negative energy of the conversation and work it into the past. "Okay, what's on the agenda tonight?"

"Drunk social-media planning!" Charisse laughs as I slide in next to her at the kitchen table. She opens her tote, which is hanging from her chair, and removes her cell phone.

Charisse is my unofficial social-media guru. She keeps me up-to-date on new trends and tells me easy things I can do throughout the week to stay relevant. Between Facebook, Instagram, Snapchat, and Twitter, I easily run out of reasons to stay in front of people. Posting about books can only take me so far. And since I don't have kids or exciting hobbies to post about, I need all the recommendations I can get.

"I have an idea," she says, holding her cell phone to her chest.

"And I told her it was a bad one and she should stay out of it," Melody interjects as she sits on the other side of the table with Aubrey in her arms.

Charisse sits up taller. "It's a *great* idea. And until you become the queen of attracting social-media followers, you have no say in my brilliance!"

"I'm insta-putty in your hands. Teach me, oh wise one." I laugh as I mock bow at her greatness.

She holds up the phone and shows me TikTok, a platform I'm still trying to figure out how to make work for my career. The hard part is, it's all videos, so I can't just go in and post a photo in two seconds and move on. I have to plan and record things. It's both fun and exhausting. Yet that's the life of an author.

"Is this like the dance you made me do last week?" I ask, looking at the screen.

"It's better. It's called the Kissing Best Friend Challenge!" She is giddy with drunk excitement.

It sounds harmless enough, so I give it a watch. The first video is a girl walking up to a guy on the beach. His back is to her, and the caption reads, *So, I wanted to try the Kissing Best Friend Challenge.*

I look up at Charisse, wildly confused. "This is a make-out thing?"

"Just keep watching. Watch, like, ten," she demands.

I look down at the screen just in time to see the girl tap the guy on the back. When he turns toward her, she stands on her toes and kisses him. She quickly backs away, laughing, but he's not. He grabs her hand and pulls her back into a heated embrace. It's so sweet.

I watch another. This one doesn't go as well. The caption starts with the girl telling us that the guy next to her has been her best friend since she was nine. She leans over and kisses him, and then he palms her in the face, pushing her away with a laugh.

I scroll through more than ten, as these videos of friends crossing the line can be super addictive. Some of them totally get into it when the guy obviously feels the same way, yet a few of them aren't into it. One says their friendship was ruined over it. That breaks my heart.

I'm a mix of emotions when the most recent video ends. The couple just laughs when it's over, and then they go in for a hug. I like this one the best.

"I'm digging it, but how can I participate? I don't have a best friend I've pined over for years." I hand Charisse her phone back.

"No, you don't, but …" Her lips grow into a shit-eating grin.

I turn to Melody, and she holds up a finger as she bounces Aubrey on her knee. "I told her it was a really bad idea."

"How bad?"

Charisse bites her lower lip. "I was thinking you could film your version of the challenge with your naughty neighbor."

A sharp laugh escapes my mouth. "Jake? Seriously?"

"See, I told you!" Melody yells out, and Aubrey hushes her mom. Melody kisses the little girl's head.

"Oh, come on. It's brilliant," Charisse defends her suggestion. "Your posts with a picture of you outperform the others, and your videos are even better. You know this will get likes, comments, and shares like crazy. You have a few thousand fans on TikTok alone, and when we did that dance last week, you had a thousand shares. You can copy and paste it to all of your accounts. You don't have to have just TikTok to enjoy it."

I pick up my drink and think about it. My first thought: *No. Fucking. Way.*

I have no idea how Jake would react if I made out with him on a whim. We're not friends like that.

Except for that one time I let him put his hands on me while he painted my body.

I still quiver at the thought.

"If I did it, I'd have to tell him first. He'd have to be one hundred percent game."

"Hell no!" Charisse yells. "You do this once, and you do it the right way. That's what makes these videos so appealing. The audience will know if he's faking it."

I pull on my lip as I think about what it would be like to kiss him. His lips alone were enough for me to use as inspiration when describing my new hero. They're so full and luscious and—

Dear me, am I really considering this?

If I did it and he was horrified, I'd have the excuse of the video challenge to use as an explanation. He would understand, and I bet he'd be willing to play along a second time once I told him. Plus, it would be cool for my heroine to kiss the guy first. I could write it with firsthand knowledge, which would definitely make it more real.

"Come on. Don't be such a wimp." Charisse playfully nudges my leg. "You can tell him before you post it, but you can't tell him before you film. It'd ruin the vibe. You know he'll be okay with it though. Men love the attention."

She's right there. This man *would* love the attention, but I hate the idea of filming him like this without him knowing.

"You're sure this is a good career move?" I take a sip and set my glass down, swirling the wine in my mouth before I swallow it. "I don't think he'd get upset, like some of those guys in the videos did," I say, more thinking out loud.

"See," Charisse says to Melody. "I knew she'd at least think about it."

"I mean, it's a bad idea, but it's not horrible. He'd totally understand that I did it for my followers. We've discussed how I have to keep up on all social-media platforms. And he's offered to help."

"You are just taking him up on his offer." Charisse nods with a smile on her face and sways her head like she's doing the *Night at the Roxbury* head dance.

"Do you have a twitch?" I look toward Melody to see if Charisse's spasms are normal.

"Go. Now. Go do it," Charisse says, nudging me toward the door.

"Now?" I open my eyes wide as my mouth drops.

"If you don't do it now, you'll think about it too much, and then you'll get inside your head and talk yourself out of it. It's like ripping a Band-Aid off. You just need to do it right away."

I turn to Melody for her advice, and she shakes her head.

"Nope, I'm not helping with this one. It's all on Drunky McDrunkster."

Shoot. Okay. I guess if this is going to happen, then there's no better time than the present.

With some liquid courage and bravado from my friend, I stand up.

"How do I look?" I ask, taking in my leggings and oversize sweatshirt.

She shakes her head, slapping her forehead with her palm. "You really need to get dressed up more often."

"What? I'm at home, doing nothing."

The two look at each other with scrunched faces, like I've offended them.

I wave them off and head toward the door. "You know what I mean. Okay, I'm going. Wish me luck."

"Your phone," Charisse yells out, and I run back to her to grab it before heading out the door.

As I knock on Jake's door, I check to make sure my

phone has enough battery. I'm tapping my foot on the floor as I knock again and wait from him to answer.

When it opens, I'm greeted by him in gray sweats and no shirt. That beautiful, glistening, tanned skin is on full display. I have to blink as I move my eyes up to his face and smile as if I wasn't just checking out his body—and the happy trail that leads below his pants.

"Hey, what's going on?" he asks, leaning against the frame.

I should have thought this through a little bit more. Smiling, I decide to not hide my intentions. Well, at least not all of them. "I was hoping you'd help me with a social-media post I wanted to do for TikTok."

"Is that the dancing app?"

"Yes. And no. There are a ton of challenges you can do, and it's super fun. Can you help me out?"

He steps back into his apartment, welcoming me inside. "Sure, come on in."

His apartment looks just like mine, except double in size. The living room, the kitchen and dining area, everything is increased in space. Plus, I'm pretty sure his has two bedrooms, where mine only has one.

It's also very well decorated—from the steel and glass furniture to the bold artwork and leather couches. Jake definitely spent more time and money decorating his place than I did.

His eyes narrow at me as his lips tilt up in a smirk. "Is there really a TikTok video, or did you just want an excuse to check out my house?"

Placing a palm on my head, I turn to him with a bashful smile. "Yes. Right. Your place is very nice, by the way." I'm a writer, and I can easily think of a lie on the fly, yet that just feels wrong. I decide to go for omission and just not say anything at all. "I need you to take a seat."

He shrugs. "Okay. Do I have to say anything?"

"Nope. Just sit down," I answer as I prop the phone on his coffee table and make sure it's getting the width of his sofa in the shot.

"You look nervous."

"I am. A little."

"Should *I* be nervous?" He's making a joke, but I don't laugh.

Instead, I just answer, "Be petrified, my friend. Because I am."

"You know, you really need to work on your pitch. You're lucky I'm pretty much game for anything because you're not making me feel at ease here." He chuckles.

Once the camera is in place, I hit record and sit next to Jake on the couch.

"Okay," I say into the camera, "I'm here with my friend Jake, who lives next door to me. He's agreed to be in this video, but I haven't told him what the video is about. So, wish me luck."

I turn to Jake and take in a deep breath. Lifting my lashes, I look up into his chocolate eyes and melt at the sight of him sitting here, staring at me, waiting to see what I'll do. His lips quirk up just a touch as he tries to figure out what I'm up to.

My tongue darts out and grazes my lower lip.

His eyes follow my movement. That chocolate turns to midnight.

I run a hand up and down my thigh, mustering up the courage. His finger twitches and hits my thigh.

I take a breath.

Here goes nothing.

Leaning forward, I arch my back, pucker my lips, and kiss him.

His lips are warm as I press mine against his, barely and briefly. As quick as I started this, I end it even faster, pulling back, my heart racing in my chest.

I take a quick inhale, and before I'm able to release it, Jake's hands wrap around my head and yank me back in.

He is kissing me.

Where my kiss was quick and vapid, his is intense and heated. His hands move from behind my head to my face, holding me in place and deepening our moment. His tongue flicks and dances against mine, passionate and powerful, as he tucks me flush against him.

I kiss him back.

My body quivers as I stroke my tongue against his, gripping him back and feeling the sensual arousal down in my core. I've written kisses. Ones where the man's hands are an embrace of her cheeks, where her skin warms when his thumb graces the curve of her jaw. I've described the way her spine tingles with the swipe of a tongue and how her body clenches with need as his lips wrap around hers.

But I've never felt it.

This is a kiss that raises the bar for all other kisses in the history of kisses.

With my hands on his chest, I feel his body—hard and strong—vibrate with a groan that has me lifting my chin. His mouth finds my jaw and places openmouthed kisses along my skin.

The break in contact is enough to have me leaning back. Our breathing is ragged as we pull away. I'm looking down, wondering how a simple kiss turned into … well, *that.*

We're nothing but labored breaths and swollen lips as I lift my head, seeing his furrowed brow as he looks at me with amused surprise.

I blink a few times, realizing what just happened.

"So, that was for TikTok?" he asks with a tilted head.

I nod.

He looks to the side and grins. "Did you get what you needed?"

I nod again.

"Are you happy with how your video turned out?"

Because I'm a woman of many words, I nod for a third time.

"I'm gonna go now." I rise from the couch and march through his apartment, out the door, and straight into my own, slamming the door and leaning against it.

"Well?" Charisse asks when she sees my expression that I'm sure is like I just saw a ghost.

"We definitely cannot post that video!" I state as I adamantly shake my head.

Melody and Charisse both stare at each other in question.

"That bad?" Charisse asks.

I hold up my hands in front of me. "I need a minute. I'm trying to figure out why the best kiss of my entire life just happened with the hot guy next door while I was fulfilling a freaking internet challenge."

A knock comes from behind me.

I freeze and listen as Jake's deep voice echoes from the other side. "You forgot your phone."

I close my eyes as I pull myself together. Outwardly, of course, because, inside, I'm a heart-pounding mess.

Pushing my shoulders back, I lift my chin and open the door as coolly and calmly as possible. Jake's standing here with a Cheshire cat grin, holding my phone out to me.

"Thanks," I say.

I'm about to close the door when he puts an arm out, keeping me from shutting it.

"And, Lace," he says, and I hold my breath. "It's called the Kissing Best Friend Challenge."

"Yeah, I know."

He grins. "We're not best friends, so I suggest, when you post it, you change the caption."

"To what?"

"*I just had the best kiss of my life with the guy who lives next door*." He winks and then turns. He heads into his apartment and closes the door gingerly.

I slide open my phone, ready to hit the Delete button on the video when I see my text messages are open. Jake forwarded the video to himself.

I close the door and turn to Melody and Charisse, who are staring at me with slack jaws and wide eyes.

That is, until Charisse throws her arms up in the air and declares, "Best. Freaking. Idea. Ever."

Melody rolls her eyes and then grins in my direction. "It was a really bad idea … but a really, *really* good one too."

I'm not only screwed. I'm also twisted.

CHAPTER TEN

Whatever my feelings are about that kiss last night—which, trust me, I have *many* feelings about that kiss—there is one thing that's for sure: it lit a fire in my belly.

Charisse and Melody left soon after, and I couldn't sleep. Hell, I couldn't sit, but I made myself.

Opening up my laptop, I stared at the screen for a mere second before I started typing.

The words flowed easily, my fingers dancing rapidly along the keys. My brain was raging like wildfire, and I couldn't type fast enough. I'd never written so much, so fast.

The characters came alive off the page. The hero is a sensitive yet charismatic artist who finds joy in the simple pleasures of life. The heroine is a schoolteacher who is afraid of being hurt again.

Their connection is intense, and their romance is pure *magic*.

I give all the credit to that kiss.

NAUGHTY NEIGHBOR

Last night, Jake ignited this thing in me. I can still taste the mint of his tongue and smell the fresh scent of his cologne. My hands burn with the touch of his heated, soft skin, and damn, my body is still reeling from the sensations that were shooting through me.

I used him as my muse. Hell, my hero's hair even morphed from brown to blond, and those blue eyes are now a chocolate brown. I praise myself for never fully explaining him in previous books so I can change him now.

I used everything I find most charming about Jake and put it in these scenes, flourishing a hero unlike any other. The literary prowess was alive last night, and I was a creative machine.

Until now.

I've hit a freaking wall.

Again.

The first time the couple met—which was epic, by the way—came easily, and their physical connection is heart-pounding. Now, I need them to start building their love connection. It's the *get to know you more than just physically* phase of the relationship. I have no idea what to have them do next.

Maybe I'm just tired. Plus, I stink from the adrenaline. I need to regroup.

In the shower, I try to think about my story line. Some ideas come to me, but they're not solid. I can picture a good scene, yet I don't know how to get there. I can't figure out how it will play into the story. Everything that's coming to me is fluff, and there's no meat there. No angst. No grit. No panic of the heart from wondering, *Will they or won't they be together?*

After my shower, I make myself some coffee—only because If I open wine I know I won't get anything done—and sit back down, pulling my laptop up to me. I read over what I wrote, as that sometimes sparks some ideas. When I get to the end of the last scene, I still have nothing.

The knock at the door stirs me from my seat. There's only one person who knocks without having to be buzzed in first, and that man just so happens to be someone I was hoping not to face today. At least, not yet. I still need time to process the state of our friendship.

As I walk to the door, I pray it's not awkward.

When I open it, I see Jake standing in the hallway. My heart instantly starts to pitter-patter just from the sight of him, but I push it aside. Friends don't make friends' hearts go pitter-patter.

"Hi," I say.

Tiny lines crinkle the sides of his eyes as he smirks. "Hey."

The first thing I look at is that cocky mouth. *Hot damn.* Then, I gaze at his hands. *Man hands.* And of course, there's that chest. *I really need to get out of the house more often.*

There's a pause between us, and I'm afraid it's going to get weird. It was a sinfully delicious kiss, but it was just a kiss. We're adults. Heck, we're even friends. We can move on like mature adult friends. Right?

Thankfully, he speaks up again, "You never posted the video."

I laugh out loud. "Are you looking for your fifteen seconds of fame?"

"Hey, I'm just here to support your career in any way I can. If I have to kiss you a thousand times so you sell books, then count me in. I want to be friends with a famous person."

"Are you just using me for my fame?" I feign shocked.

"Absolutely. When they make a movie of your book, I'm going to be on the red carpet. I look really good in a tux."

"Well, since the fate of the world seeing you in a tux is on the line, then I suppose I could post the video. Just for you though." I grin in his direction as I walk away to grab my phone. He enters my apartment behind me. "Do you have social media? I can tag you."

"I have Facebook, which I don't use often. I get why you like it though. It's a great way to interact with your readers. I'm sure they love it."

"I've made some great friends on the amazing World Wide Web."

I upload the video while neither of us says a word.

When I post it, I glance back up at him, and he grins.

"Are you hungry? I was just about to head out for something to eat. Want to join me?"

I take a deep breath in and nod my head. "You know what? An early dinner sounds like a great idea. Just give me twenty minutes."

His face lights up when I say yes, but I try not to read into it. Dinner with a friend might help clear my head right now with work and set us back on the right track in our relationship.

I do a quick blowout of my hair and add some makeup. Taking a cue from his jeans and button-down,

I slide on a pair of ripped jeans, a sleeveless tank, and ballet flats, grabbing a light jacket before we exit my apartment together.

We head down the street to an Italian place that I love. It's super casual with counter-style ordering. I select the ravioli while he peruses the menu for a while before deciding on a sausage sandwich. With a bottle of Chianti, we grab a seat on their patio outside.

As he pours my glass, he asks, "So, how's the book coming along?"

"Really well actually."

"Glad to hear it."

"What about you? No hot date lined up tonight?"

"I thought you were my date," he teases.

"If I were your date, I most definitely would have dressed nicer."

"You mean, like put on a little gold dress?"

I press my fingers to my forehead and groan. "Please don't remind me about the worst date in history. I don't go out with a guy in years, and when I do, it's a waste of a perfectly good dress."

He grins. "Let's not mourn the dress too much. I'm sure we can revitalize it. I'd be happy to take you dancing."

"Hmm, I see. You'll only take me out if I get all dressed up. I know your type, Jake Moreau. I've seen the women who come traipsing in and out of your apartment. You have definitely gone for the same kind of girl."

"First, I'm out with you this very minute. Second, you've looked the same since I first met you, and I still come around. Obviously, looks aren't a big deal to me."

NAUGHTY NEIGHBOR

My eyes open wide in shock at the way he just said that.

He shakes his head, letting out a big laugh. "That did not sound as bad in my head. I promise."

"It kind of did, but you're off the hook. I don't have an aversion to loungewear."

"And that did *not* distract me from enjoying that kiss last night."

I scrunch my eyes closed in embarrassment. "Is it possible for us to ignore that?"

"For now. But not forever." He laughs, and I peek an eye open to see his charming grin. "I'll let you off the hook under one condition: you tell me why you haven't gone out with a man in years."

I groan. Of the two topics—talking about my ambush kiss or talking about Michael—I'm having a hard time choosing the least cringeworthy.

"I moved to the city with my college sweetheart, only to have him ditch me for an Insta yoga instructor."

"Is that why you never date? Besides that last guy who—"

"Was a complete ass and reminded me why I don't trust men. That would be correct."

"Not all men are slime. Some can be quite chivalrous."

"I can't seem to find the rare few. How can you tell the difference between the good ones and those who just want to get in your pants?"

"Trust me, all men want to get in your pants. We're pretty simple that way. It's just a matter of if you're okay with it being casual or if you want something more. In that case, it's key to communicate that to the man you're seeing." His lips twist to the side while his eyebrows pinch together. "I take it, there have been no one-night stands in your life?"

I shake my head while I take a bite of my ravioli. "Nope."

"And you're how old?" he asks with surprise.

"Why is that so hard to believe? Sorry I've never met a guy and slept with him right away." I laugh.

He nods slowly. "I have. I mean, with a woman, that is. Does that make you look at me differently?"

A sharp laugh escapes my lips. "You do realize, I live next door to you, and our walls aren't as thick as they should be. There's not much you can hide from me. Even the first time I met you, you were walking a girl out after a sleepover."

His shoulders fall like it's something he's suddenly ashamed of. I try to stop his reaction.

"Hey, what you do with all of that"—I motion my hand up and down his body—"is your choice. No judgment here. I love sex. Really, I do. I'm just picky about who I have it with."

"Because they might leave you for an Insta yoga instructor."

"Among other things." I stab a ravioli and pop it into my mouth. "Tell me, where do you find these girls?"

He gives me a deadpan stare. "You act like I run a brothel from my house. There hasn't been that many girls."

I give him the same stare. "You're testing the waters while you find the future Mrs. Moreau. What do you do?"

He takes a bite of his food and sits back in his chair like he's really thinking about it. "I guess it all depends.

I don't want you to think I'm this guy who goes out, searching for girls just to get laid."

"All men are simpleminded creatures though."

I'm laughing at my joke, but he's not. His look is stoic and kind of wistful.

"I would like to settle down someday, contrary to what my mom says. I just haven't met the right woman yet."

"Then, maybe you're looking in the wrong places," I say before taking a sip of my wine.

He purses his lips and nods, staring straight into my eyes. "I'm beginning to think the same thing."

A shiver runs down my spine at the sound of his deep, husky voice.

"Let me ask you this then. If you did meet this woman, what is the perfect date? You said, it's all about showing that you listen to what they want. Where do you take a woman when you're ready to show her what *you* want?

Waving a finger, he laughs. "Oh no, I'm not giving away my secrets."

My mouth forms an O in amusement. "It's a secret, you say? Now, I'm intrigued."

"A man never reveals his hidden corners of the world."

Crossing my legs, I stare off to the side in enjoyment and then look back with a non-convinced shake of my head. "It's probably something like a little French bistro off the beaten path."

"Where the owner plays the accordion and sings in his foreign tongue?"

I lift my glass to him. "Knew it! You're so easy to peg."

He shakes his head with a laugh. "That's not it at all."

"Then, you don't really have a place. If you did, you'd be gloating about it right now. The most romantic spot in all of Chicago, just for you and that special girl."

"You think you know me so well, don't you?"

"I had you marked the first day I saw you in that towel."

The mention of the day we met has him lifting a brow. "Think about that often, do you?"

I turn away because I hate lying while looking someone in the eye. "Never."

A wicked grin graces his lips as he leans forward. "What are you doing tomorrow night?"`

"Working. Beyond office hours. I have pages to send to my agent by Friday."

"Call it a day at eight. After that, you're mine."

Now, it's my turn to quirk a brow. "Huh?"

"We're going on a date, Lace."

CHAPTER ELEVEN

On the shore of Lake Michigan is the dome-shaped concrete building of the Adler Planetarium. I'm not sure what time the planetarium is open, but from experience, museums are always closed by six. What he plans on doing around here is beyond me.

"Are we going for a walk?" I look out at the cityscape in the foreground.

"No. We're going inside."

"There are no cars in the lot. Pretty sure this place is closed."

His expression splits into the biggest smile. "You *are* pretty. And you are correct."

"I knew you were trouble, Moreau, but breaking and entering? I didn't think you had it in you."

He laughs as he gets out of the car. "You really do have an active imagination."

I follow him up the steps of the historic building.

His excitement as we approach the planetarium is enough to pull at my heartstrings.

A gentleman in a pair of khaki pants and a red polo opens the door, greeting Jake warmly.

"Lacey, this is my buddy Kent. He's a telescope facilitator."

"There are few people who I'd give a private viewing to, and this guy is one of them," Kent says with a smile.

Jake leans in. "He's only being nice because I'm giving him the friends-and-family discount on his wedding arrangements."

Kent laughs. "My fiancée has very expensive taste."

We walk inside and follow Kent through a uniquely shaped hall with vibrant lighting and interactive, motion-sensing displays. He gives us a mini tour of the facility. It's fun to roam around the exhibits without a map and have the information explained to us as we walk. We can't see everything because Kent is only able to open certain parts, but what we're viewing is spectacular. I crane my neck as I stare at giant replicas of the planets hanging from the ceiling.

When we get to a display that shows us the Chicago night sky, Kent leaves us alone to explore on our own.

I turn to Jake. "There's an episode of *Friends* where Ross takes Rachel on an after-hours date to the planetarium. It's my favorite."

"I'm no Ross Geller, but I do know a thing or two about stars." He walks with his hands behind his back as we look around. "You can see forty-five hundred stars with the naked eye. And what we see are images that have traveled light-years. Many of the stars we see today might not even be there anymore."

"Seriously?"

"We're seeing the reflection of the sun bouncing off the stars, but they are so far away, and light only travels so fast that we're actually seeing a reflection from years ago. They might still be there just like we see, but many have already exploded. We don't know yet."

"That's really fascinating." I follow him as he points out different star maps.

"This month, if you look south or southwest, Jupiter and Saturn are readily visible. You probably wouldn't even know you were looking at them. Jupiter is the brighter of the two. If you can find it, you'll see the constellation Sagittarius, and next to it is the S-shaped Scorpius. And this reddish star is Antares. It's the heart of Scorpius."

He's adorably nerdy about the subject. I shouldn't say it's surprising because he's always come off as an intelligent man. Yet a man who can read the stars is more well-traveled in my mind than those who have read a thousand books.

"How do you know so much about the night sky?"

"I love astronomy. My mom is really into astrology. She took me here a lot when I was little. They were doing a live viewing of Saturn's rings, and I was mesmerized. I remember thinking, *How is that even possible?* I could visibly see the ring that wraps around it, just as I'd seen it in books. Made it all real, I guess."

"I can imagine, that would be pretty cool."

"For years, I wanted to be an astronaut." He shakes his head, chuckling to himself. "I went to space camp in grade school. What I would have given up back then to go up in space. If it felt that cool, seeing it through a telescope, could you imagine what seeing it in person, clear as day in front of you, would be like?"

"There's a ride at Epcot for that."

He laughs out loud. "I'll have to go there someday. Maybe you can take me." He grins as he nudges my shoulder.

We walk side by side out of the exhibit and into another.

"What changed your dream of becoming an astronaut?"

"I was always told the flower shop would be mine someday. I had to keep on with the family tradition." He lowers his voice like he's repeating words he's heard a million times. "Every Moreau has worked there since 1923. My great-grandfather peddled flowers from his farm and sold them on the streets as a side hustle when his first business went under during the first World War."

"No Moreau can veer from the family plan?"

"Sure we can. Even though they used to work there, my sister, Milène, is an architect, and Penelope is a schoolteacher. I come from an old-school family. My grandfather left it to his oldest son, and my father is leaving it to me."

"And you don't want it?"

"To be honest?" He pauses as a grin covers his face. "Of course I do. I love it. One, working in a business with a legacy like ours is an honor. And the work, well, I get to make everyone's day. Even in the darkest of times, flowers put a smile on your face. It's the only gift you can give when a life is brought into the world and also when one is taken away. If you want to say you're sorry, do it with a purple hyacinth, and to show your love—"

"Say it with a red rose."

"Or if you come to me, I'll tell you to give daisies." He grins, and I tilt my head in interest. "They're actually made of two flowers. The yellow middle is considered one flower, and the white outer ring is technically another, but together, they become one."

Be still my heart, which is thumping pretty sweetly right now.

"A man who can talk stars and flowers. Maybe you're right. You are definitely hero material."

"Glad you're finally realizing it." He waggles his brows. "I'm glad you posted that video. By the comments, I think we did a pretty good job."

I laugh out loud, surprised he brought it up. He's right though. I've never had so much engagement on a post.

My smile lingers. "Yeah, my readers seem to think you're pretty hot."

"It's about fucking time." That cocky grin flashes as he faces me. "Wanna see something extraordinary?"

His eyes crinkle with the lightness in his expression. It's the kind of look that makes you want to follow him off a cliff. If he said jump, I totally would.

With my hand in his, Jake leads me to the Doane Observatory within the Adler Planetarium. He waves to a man in a small window up high, and I recognize Kent's face. Jake and I take seats in the middle row of the theater.

"I've never seen a show like this before."

"I told him to mute the narration and just play the music. It's far more enjoyable this way."

"I trust you." It's not a lie. So far, this has been the most unique and enjoyable date I've ever been on even if it is just to prove a point that he knows how to take a girl out.

The lights go black, and the ceiling ignites in a spectacular soiree of visual scenes. The Milky Way galaxy is in view. We zoom closer and closer until we're in the orbits of the solar system.

Hauntingly beautiful mood music plays over the loudspeaker as we travel around the sun and leap from one planet to the next. The room rumbles as we move through light-years, and there's a whoosh of air I can feel on my cheek.

His hand moves closer to mine as the red rocks of Mars come into view. His knee grazes my leg when we pass the red spot of Jupiter. The heat of his body presses against mine as we weather the storms of Uranus. He tells me Venus is named after the Roman goddess of love and beauty. And when we get to Saturn, he shows me the rings of water and ice that stole his heart when he was just a boy.

I could listen to him talk about the universe all night. His explanations are simple, his jokes are amusing, and his expressions as he discusses things makes him absolutely mesmerizing.

That's when I realize I stopped watching the show.

I'm watching him.

His mouth is parted, his eyes are hooded, and his body is filled with a calm, as if this is exactly where he wants to be.

And then he looks at me.

My breath hitches because the light in his eyes is still there. Except, instead of talking about flowers or his beloved stars, he's looking at me. I feel like he's the sun and I'm orbiting around him. There's no doubt that I could soak in his stare for the rest of my life.

He leans forward, and my heart picks up. "If I kiss you right now, without a camera rolling, would you mind?"

I instinctively lick my lips as I take a sharp breath in, and my words fail me.

His head dips lower until his lips are mere inches from mine. "Would you?"

"No," I whisper back.

He places a hand on my cheek, leans forward, and kisses me. It's soulful and sweet. Intense and delicious. I wasn't prepared for the intensity of his kiss last time, but today, I'm ready to devour and savor every moment.

With the planets and the sun dancing on the sky above us, our tongues dance in a rhythm all of their own as our breaths become one. I feel his touch down to my core, and there's no part of me that wants him to stop.

I slide my hand into his thick, dirty blond hair and pull him in closer. His left arm tightens around my back as he brings me into him, his tongue stroking between my lips, sending tingles straight between my legs.

He pulls away from my lips but places his forehead to mine.

"You win," I whisper. "Your secret first-date place is pretty amazing."

"I told you I had moves."

"I'll never doubt you again."

He laughs as he puts an arm around me, pulling me into his side and staring up at the show.

"Thanks for coming with me," he says.

I nod. "Thanks for inviting me. This is fun."

He grins. "It sure is."

I bite my lower lip, stopping myself from kissing him again. He smirks, and I know he can tell.

We finish the show and then bid goodnight to Kent. On the ride home, Jake plays more of that music that was on in the planetarium, and we listen as we drive along the shoreline, staring at the Windy City. Its colors of pinks, purples, and golds illuminate the darkened water, making it look absolutely stunning.

When we get home, he walks me to my door, kisses me softly on the cheek, and slowly backs up toward his place.

"Night," I say before turning around, entering my apartment, and closing the door.

So many emotions are running through me. My heart is pounding, and I can't control the smile on my face. I only get this exhilarated when I write. It's a feeling of happiness I can't control. To me, it's better than any drug or alcohol.

That's when the words drown me.

I race to my computer, open it up, and let it pour out. One after another, my fingers glide across the keyboard as my best writing spills onto the page.

CHAPTER TWELVE

I burned the midnight oil and some of the morning's as well. It felt amazing, and then I crashed—hard.

My head doesn't want to leave the pillow, except my buzzer is going off, which means I have a visitor from the outside world.

I roll over and answer my phone, my voice groggy, "Who is it?"

"It's your mother," she sings into the receiver.

I punch in the number nine and listen as the buzzing sound chimes in the receiver. Knowing she must be inside by now, I push the covers off the bed and make my way over to the front door, unlocking it and leaving it ajar as I walk to the Keurig.

"You look well rested," she states in a serious tone, which is really her humor, exaggerating the state of a situation.

I pop a pod in. "What are you doing in the city?"

"I have two grant proposals in schools nearby. I told you about this."

I try to rack my mind to remember her saying she'd be in the city. "Sorry. I've been a little all over the place this week in my attempt to finish up this book. I've finally hit my stride, and I'm on target to finish by my deadline."

A closed-mouth smile graces her face. "What's this one about? Another billionaire or a handsome prince?"

I narrow my eyes at her comment and wait as my cup fills. It's too early—well, considering it's afternoon, it's too late—to find a witty comeback. I need my liquid stamina first.

"Or a strapping doctor with green eyes who wants to fill the heroine's belly with a baby?" she muses as she takes in my bookshelf and the spines of romances, including my own.

"He's from a wealthy family," I state, and she makes that hum of disapproval. "And an artist, so he's pretty much a prince in my eyes."

The cup fills to the top, and I grab it, soaking in the heat.

She sets her tote bag on the table and takes a seat. "I'll have a cup too. Thank you for asking."

"Sorry. That was rude of me. French roast alright?"

Mom nods as she folds her hands on the table. "I haven't heard from you in a few days. Everything good?"

"Yes, actually. I went on a date."

"A date?" Her expression is a mixture of delighted and horrified as I put her mug in front of her and take a seat at the table.

"Two actually. A really bad one and a really good

one. Funny, I haven't gone out in years, and I went on two dates in a week. Guess I'm making up for lost time."

"Should I be concerned?" She raises her eyebrows over her mug with a tilt to her lips.

I smile to myself as I brush my fingers along my lips, the kiss I shared with Jake lingering on them. "Don't worry, Mom. I still don't believe in real life happily ever afters."

"You make me sound like I'm the evil queen, set to erase romantic love from the human experience. I'm just concerned that you have these grand illusions of what a man should be. When you idolize a man, he only lets you down."

"I'm not idolizing anyone, trust me."

She takes a sip from her cup. "You write about things that don't really happen. It's not every day that a single mom runs into a billionaire who sweeps her off her feet."

I grin because even though my mom hates the tropes of my books, she reads every one. Never once has she critiqued my writing style, which is why I entertain these conversations. In fact, she applauds it. It's the characters she has issues with.

"Clearly, I know the odds of a bazillionaire—dominant in the bedroom yet sensitive in matters of the heart with a dark past that only *I*, the Converse-sneaker-wearing virgin, can heal the wounds of—swooping in on his private jet and whisking me away are low to nonexistent."

"Well, that's a mouthful." She shakes her head with a slight laugh while taking a sip.

"People like to abandon their reality. If I wrote

about a guy who comes home, cracks open a beer, and watches baseball with his hand down his pants, they'd D-N-F me." When she lifts a brow, I further explain, "Do not finish."

She sighs. "Do you ever feel like you're filling these women's hearts with hope of things that will never come true? What about the one who reads a book and then looks at her husband and thinks, *He's no Christian Grey. I want a Christian in my life. Not this*?"

"Are you admitting you read *Fifty Shades of Grey*?"

With a swipe of her hand in the air, she explains, "I'm not the only person who feels fairy tales only hurt society. We need to lift these women up and tell them what life is really like, not lie to them."

"So, I should write about dirtbags? Or better yet, date one?"

"Dear, no. However, if a man presents himself as one of these impressive heroes—who don't really exist— then he's a loser because he's only pretending."

I consider her words. All men are going to present themselves in their best light. During my two dates, each man started off being a gentleman. Only one stayed that way to the end. While I agree with her—and I always have—I'm starting to wonder if she'd ever give someone a chance again to make it to the end of the date.

"Do you think all men are losers?" I ask.

"No. Of course I know there are decent men. But in relationships, you must be wary. Men are incapable of monogamy."

"Just because you got a bad deal from my father doesn't mean all men are like that."

She folds her arms across her body and taps her

foot. "*Michael* definitely wasn't a good deal either. Case in point of a man who pretends to be the hero when he's really a zero."

Our conversation has just crossed a line, and we both know it. I stand up, needing the space away from her and the mention of Michael.

"Clearly, I know there's no such thing as the perfect man. And while I thank you for being concerned about my views on the male species and the perception of romantic love, I am more than aware of what the reality is like. The reason I'm single has nothing to do with the heroes I write."

"Oh, I'm aware. It's your good-for-nothing father." She sighs. "Come on now. I didn't come over here to start a fight with you on our perception of the opposite sex. Men will be men. They're hunters by nature. Take Jackie and JFK for example. They were America's couple. She was a woman we were all meant to look up to, and her husband cheated on her left and right. I'll never understand how she was supposed to just accept it, yet she did."

I walk to the kitchen, needing more coffee almost as much as I need a reprieve. It's hard to think she's right. I have to believe she's not. There has to be men out there who are as good as the men I write in my books.

I take my refilled mug and walk to the living room. "Did Dad cheat on you?"

"There's no reason to talk about what he did or didn't do."

"You've never really told me much. I think I should know more about him now that I'm older."

"There's nothing really to know, except that he left

us. We were together for a little over a year when I found out I was pregnant with you. He said he didn't want anything to do with you. So, we broke up, and I had you nine months later. He came back for a few years and then one day decided the nuclear family wasn't something he wanted."

"How did you two meet?"

"We met in college. We had a class together. He wanted to eventually move to LA, and you know I never want to leave the Midwest. It's my home. You were five when he decided to make a go of it as an actor."

"Did you ever try to reconnect with him?"

She shakes her head. "I didn't want anything to do with a man who didn't want to love his child. Believe me, it was for the best. He's living on the West Coast, trying to live the California dream. He got what he wanted, and I got what I wanted." She scoots closer and places her hand on mine. "This is reality. There are a lot of unhappy people living in marriages that are horrible only because it's what society tells them they have to do. I'm here to say, you don't have to have a man to get everything you want."

Her hand squeezing mine makes me content with how my life has turned out. I might not have a present father, but my mother's dedication is everything. That's why I have to make sure she is honest about what she wants in life.

"Are you ever lonely? Do you ever miss having someone by your side? Someone to curl up and watch a movie with or just to make dinner with every night?"

She sits back and tilts her head. "Of course. People need companionship for sure. But this notion that you need to be with another person for the rest of your life is archaic."

"A person needs intimacy though."

"Friendships are conducive to a healthy mental state, married or not. It's the people you surround yourself with who matter most. You're a prime example. Look at your life. Between your work, the people you meet at these book signings and conventions, your socialization … you seem to be doing just fine by yourself."

I am doing just fine, and yet the words sting my soul.

She's right. I am doing *fine* on my own.

I'm also turning into her. I'm at odds with if that's a good or bad thing.

A knock on my door, thankfully, takes me out of my downward spiral. I put my mug on the table and walk to the door.

Jake is there, holding a plate of brownies. "Thought you could use a sugar boost," he says with the sweetest grin.

"Who's that?" my mom calls out.

I take the brownies from him. "I'd run if I were you."

Jake looks around my shoulder, and his eyes widen at the sight of my mom. He's met her once before in the hallway about a year ago, and he knows she can be a bit intense. By intense, I mean, she asked him a thousand questions about his personal life, sex life, work life, and where he stood on politics. I didn't know him well enough, so when I saw she had cornered him, I hid in the hall, too mortified to make an appearance until he escaped and I heard Mom's footsteps coming my way.

"Who's there?" Mom asks again, walking toward the door.

I move to the side, so she can see. "You remember my neighbor, Jake."

She waves him over and holds an arm out for him to take a seat. "Come in! Join our conversation."

"About what?" he asks with a furrowed brow.

"You don't want to be part of this," I explain as he crosses the threshold.

"Nonsense." My mom waves me off. "We were just discussing how men are probably better off with roaming through life rather than being held down to one woman."

With an ease in his walk, he heads inside and takes a seat on my sofa. "I'm intrigued."

"I was telling Lacey how her books give women false notions of romance."

"How so?" he asks.

"With my books filled with fluff and romance, Mom thinks I'm filling their heads with fantasy when I should be handing them reality."

"Your mom does have a point," he says, turning to me. "My sister Penelope has watched *The Notebook* a thousand times, and she's still waiting for her real-life Noah to build her a house as an undying testament of his love and affection."

"See?" Mom says with a cheeky grin.

"However"—he pivots toward Mom—"my mother and sisters love Lacey's words, and I think they're better for reading them," Jake says proudly as he sits a little taller, like he's protective of me.

"They read my books?" I ask him, not sure how I feel about his mom reading my words.

He grins. "Yeah. After you came by the shop, my mom bought them each a copy on Amazon, and they read together, like a mini book-club thing. You have three new fans."

"You said you think they're better for reading her books?" she asks him.

"My mother gave me an earful about it while we were at the shop. She thinks Lacey is brilliant."

"Really?" I ask, turning to him, surprised and completely touched.

"Milène too. Penelope read three of your books in as many days. That girl is already cyberstalking you on social media, so beware when your inbox blows up with love notes."

"I'll consider myself warned." I chuckle under my breath.

Jake crosses his leg over his knee and engages my mother in conversation. "I don't know or understand the female brain, but I think, with romance—particularly the books that Lacey writes—it helps women escape the reality of kids and work and household chores and brings them back to what it was like when they first met their husbands. At least that's what my sister said. It reminded her of the good days and how that love is still there even if it's buried somewhere in the craziness of life. As for my other sister who is single, I think it will give her hope, albeit a false sense in some ways, but at least she has that notion that love is out there."

My smile is a mile wide as I listen to him speak.

"I like you, Jake. You're very diplomatic. I'd love to know, why aren't you married?"

He makes a pretend gesture, as if he's going to get up and leave because the conversation turned uncomfortable, then takes his seat again. "I just haven't found the right woman."

"Picky?" she asks.

"Very," he states with a laugh. "I'm not the type to settle, so I'm waiting until I'm with the right girl."

His eyes meet mine, and I instantly take a drink from my mug, which is now empty.

"Looking for the right woman … so in the meantime, you're having a blast with all the wrong ones?" Mom chuckles.

He grins. "There's nothing wrong with that. I don't string anyone along. I date and dare-I-say I've even loved a few. But I've never been *in* love. If I don't feel like I can make that life-long commitment, then I make sure to let them know."

Mom snaps her fingers and points one at me. "That. Have you ever written a character who treats women like that?"

I turn toward my computer and grimace. I have actually. As in right now. My hero is a romantic who refuses to settle, so he's dating his way around the city, waiting for the perfect woman.

In this moment, I realize just how much of my hero has been based off of not only my interactions with Jake lately, but also him in general.

"Maybe I should hang out with Jake more often to get some inspiration," I say.

"That sounds like a plan." He swings his arm over the back of the sofa.

The three of us spend the next hour talking about all the *real* men I should be writing. I'm laughing so hard at the crazy ideas Mom and Jake come up with together. From Bill, the flatulent barber, to Chaz, the guy who sits in his living room and talks to his parakeet all day, only to hear the words, "Yes, master."

I'm wiping tears from my eyes as I refill our coffee mugs.

After awhile, Mom looks at her phone and says she has to leave for her appointment. She bids us farewell, leaving Jake and me alone.

"That was an interesting afternoon," I tell him as we walk to my door.

"Your mom is pretty funny when she lets her hair down."

"No. That was all you. You make people laugh, and you become instant best friends with them."

His eyes crinkle at my compliment. "It's easier to play nice than to argue."

"Well, I'm kind of a hothead, so that philosophy doesn't come easy. It's an art."

"Hey"—he levels his gaze with mine and takes a serious tone—"speaking of art, I know we were having fun just now, but I want you to know that I think you're brilliant."

My smile falls. "You read more of my books, didn't you?"

"Of course I did. You're my favorite author."

I swallow, touched by the notion that he sought my work out and from the compliment.

"Do you think I romanticize my heroes?"

"I think for someone who pretends she doesn't believe in love, deep down, you know it burns brighter and hotter than you've ever experienced." He places the softest of kisses on my cheek and backs up toward his door. "Now, go back to work, Lacey girl. You have a deadline."

CHAPTER THIRTEEN

"I love it! Every single word. Damn, girl. I'm all over the place with how excited I am for this book. When do I get the rest?" Wendy utters the words I've been dying to hear since I started this series.

After months of writer's block, of trying and trying to get a story together, I managed to pump out half a book in a week.

It's Jake. I know it. The man has inspired me more than I can explain. Actually, I haven't explained it to him. His ego will probably get in the way.

"I'm going to start making beta notes for this," Wendy continues. "I have some suggestions, but all in all, this is addictive. I need the rest of the story. Can you schedule the editor for the end of the month?"

"I wasn't planning on publishing until January, so I scheduled editing for December."

"December?" She sounds horrified. "My contact at Winston Arms said they want to have their talent signed by the end of the year for next year. This baby needs to release in November."

"That's too soon."

"December sales tank, honey. You know you can't release anything, except for a Christmas novella, around the holidays."

"I know. I just—"

"You are a top contender, and I don't want you to miss out on this opportunity. I need the final in two weeks."

I gulp. "Fourteen days?"

"That's what I said. You got this!"

"I know. It's just so fast. I still have to get it edited and—"

"I'm here for you. Like I said, I'm making notes. We'll polish it up and then do a quick edit before submission."

I take a deep breath in, internally pumping myself up. "I can do this. Two weeks, and you'll have your story."

"Amazeballs. I'm so happy for you. Now, go write!"

She laughs as we hang up, and I fall onto my couch. The writing has been flowing so much that I haven't made my normal plot list of what's going to happen in each chapter.

I thought I could take a few days to let everything settle in and think about the story, but knowing I need to get it finished right away means I have to abandon my usual methods. I'm not sure what to do next, so I think of the one thing that has helped me this entire time.

Jake.

JEANNINE COLETTE & LAUREN RUNOW

I walk into the hall and over to his apartment and knock.

"What's up, Lace?" he says after opening the door with a big smile on his face.

"Do you want to hang out with me today?"

He chuckles at my bluntness, and I inhale, reminding myself to calm down and not be so stressed. "Sure. Where do you want to go?"

I pinch my brows together. "Actually, I have no idea." Because I don't. *That's why I'm standing here, looking for ideas.* "I haven't been to any place trendy or exciting in a long time. How about Navy Pier?"

"That's a tourist trap."

"I know. Charisse says the same thing. That's why I've never gone." I look to the side as I try to think of something else.

"Wait, wait, wait. You've never been to Navy Pier?" He gives me a dumbfounded expression. "Put on a sweater. We're going out."

"Stop. Rewind. I was the one asking you out."

"Oh. That's right. By all means." He opens his arms out wide, inviting me to ask him.

I plaster a big grin on my face. "Put on a sweater, Jake. We're going out."

Without a doubt, Navy Pier is Chicago's top attraction. Stretching into Lake Michigan, the pier houses a bustling array of activities, including rides, games, restaurants, boat tours, and Centennial Wheel, a Ferris wheel standing at one hundred and ninety-six feet.

As we get out of our Uber, we're welcomed by the U-shaped sign at the foot of the pier. Group tours are all gathered in their meeting locations to the right while families walk in, corralling their kids, and couples leisurely stroll hand in hand.

"Welcome to Navy Pier," Jake sings out, opening his arms out wide. "What should we do first?"

"I want to ride that!" I point up at the Ferris wheel with its navy-blue gondolas lined with wall-to-wall glass.

He pulls up his wrist to check his watch. "Well, it's six o'clock, and the sun will be going down in about an hour or so. Why don't we walk around first and then go to the wheel? The view from up top is pretty cool at night."

I bounce my shoulders up and down. "I like your style. Lead the way, my good man."

Holding out my elbow, I offer him to take it. He eyes me curiously and then slides his arm through mine and gives it a tug.

We stroll through the pier. I pull him into one of the shops, and he follows me around as I look at the trinkets. Then, I stand by as he tries on designer sunglasses at another.

Everywhere we go, Jake knows someone. He gets stopped by a friend from high school as we walk past a carousel, and then while standing outside a tropical garden, he talks to a couple he worked with, doing centerpieces for their wedding. We stop and watch a street performer create a painting, using various objects. Jake is enamored with the creation, so we wait until it is complete, and then he praises the man for a few minutes about his craft.

As the wind blows over the pier, I curl my arms around myself and rub my forearms. Jake notices and slings his arm around me, pulling me close and kissing the top of my head.

When we hear music pouring out from the Beer Garden, we head on over and grab beers, and I watch him ponder over the menu for ten minutes.

"I'm gonna get a burger," I announce to him as I put my menu on the table.

He's playing with his lower lip as he scours the list. "The beer-soaked brats here are amazing, but so are the nachos. And I haven't had a burger in a while."

I shake my head and watch the band play. "Take your time."

A few minutes later, a waitress comes over to take our order. Jake still looks conflicted.

I laugh. "Are you always this indecisive?"

"About food? Yes," he confesses.

I take the menu from him and hand it to the waitress. "We'll take a bratwurst, nachos, and a burger to share."

She writes the order down and walks away while Jake looks at me like I saved his life.

"What if I don't want to share my meal with you?" he asks with a smile.

I shrug. "We ordered three. By the time you decide which one you want, I'll be done with my half of the burger."

He waggles a finger at me. "I could use a woman like you in my life."

"Good thing I'm right next door." I take a swig of my beer and settle back into my seat.

We listen to the music, drink our beers, and devour our food.

While we eat, Jake tells me jokes, and I laugh like a fool.

"You hid under Milène's bed in a Freddy Krueger mask?" I ask in disbelief.

"I waited for an hour until she finally got in bed. I almost fell asleep myself."

"She must have died."

"As soon as she turned the lights off, I popped out and shouted. She screamed so loud that my parents came bustling in," he says with a laugh. "She wouldn't sleep in her room for a month."

I laugh into the back of my hand. "You're a horrible brother."

He holds up a hand in agreement. "The worst. But adorable."

"An adorable master trickster."

"That doesn't count the time I cut the bristles off her toothbrush, threw water balloons at her and her friends from my bedroom window when they were on the trampoline, or wrapped every single piece of makeup that she had in wrapping paper and an absurd amount of tape."

I shake my head, not believing some of these stories. "The girls must have hated you."

"Only Milène. Penelope was my baby. I never pranked her." He takes a sip of his beer and then lifts a finger, as if he just remembered something. "Except for one time. I wrapped her in cellophane and made her into a baby burrito. Her body only. Not her head, of course."

"Of course."

"She loved it. Mom, not so much."

"I can only imagine."

As an only child, I enjoy hearing his stories about growing up in a full household. Not that mine lacked in any way. In fact, being the sole focus of a woman who felt her daughter needed to see the world for what it was meant a lot of road trips.

"Thirty-nine states," I say proudly. "I have a road map ready to conquer the last eleven. Five on the West Coast and six on the East."

"What is your favorite city?"

"Wow. That's a hard one. I loved certain ones at different times in my life. As a little kid, it was Orlando because Disney World is the most magical place on earth."

"Why do I have a hard time envisioning your mother at the Magic Kingdom?"

"Don't let her fool you. She has certain views on life that make her seem hard, but she was fun when I was growing up. Anything I wanted to do, we did, and anything she wanted me to see, I went willingly. We were a great team."

The sides of his eyes crinkle. "I get that."

"Indianapolis was awesome because they have the largest children's museum in the world. In high school, I fell in love with Philadelphia because I was a huge history nerd. In college, I went to DC for a Women's March, making it one of my favorite experiences. But I have to say, my all-time favorite city is Traverse City."

145

He looks like he's going to spit out his beer. "Michigan?"

I laugh at his reaction. "Yep."

"Wait. Not New York, Miami, Boston, San Francisco—"

"No to all. They're really cool, and trust me, I would not turn my nose up at a weekend away to Manhattan, but there's something about Traverse City that hits my soul. It's a four-season playground. In the summer, the beaches are gorgeous, and there's so much to do outdoors. The cherry blossoms in the spring are magnificent, and the fall leaves are amazing. And the winter leaves these blankets of snow everywhere. Plus, the town is quaint yet bustling with things to do. I don't know … it's like it has the best of everything."

"Have you ever considered moving there?"

"No. Illinois is home, and my mom is here. I could never go too far. We're all each other has."

"Probably for the better. That's a city for outdoorsy people. No offense, but I don't take you for the outdoorsy type."

I laugh with a nod. "You're observant. I might not like to hike or ski or any of that. I do like to sit and watch. A spectator."

"Oh, really? And what have you thought about me?"

"This feels like a trap." I sit back in my seat, eyeing him suspiciously.

"I promise I won't be upset by anything you say."

I bite my lip and consider his request. "Like your mom said, you're a typical Libra. You're the life of the party, and while you have a Rolodex of friends, you enjoy stopping by my apartment because there's something about hanging with an introvert like me that you find soothing," I pause to make sure I'm not offending him in any way before I continue, "You're very stylish, and you enjoy the finer things in life. Case in point: your trendy T-shirt costs more than my entire outfit. Which makes me wonder why you do things like come to Navy Pier with me."

"I don't look like a Navy Pier kind of guy?"

"Um, no."

"So, why do you think I'm here now?"

"Because you're a people-pleaser. You'll do anything to put the company you keep at ease."

The corner of his mouth tilts with an appreciative smile. The wind lifts my hair and flips it in front of my face.

He leans forward and brushes it back, pushing it behind my ear. "Let's get you up in that wheel."

We make our way to Centennial Wheel and wait in the long line. I offer to leave because of the wait time, but Jake takes it in stride. We laugh and joke as we inch forward, making the time go fast until it's our turn to board.

Taking a seat across from him, I marvel at the glass enclosure that gives a panoramic view of the lake ahead and the skyline behind me. The ride slides forward just enough to let other passengers on in the gondolas following us.

The car starts to move, and my belly swims with anticipation. I'm all for trying new things, but heights aren't my favorite. Looking down, I see the Tilt-A-Whirl ride and wonder if we should have tried that instead.

"You okay over there?" he asks when he sees my wary expression.

"Yeah. Just a little anxious. Not the biggest fan of heights. I was hoping the enclosure would make me feel more protected."

"Not doing the trick?" he asks as the car jolts, rising to the top.

"No. But I'll be good. I might be nervous, but I don't back down from fear easily."

He flashes a smile. "That might be what I like most about you."

"Mmhmm," I utter as I look down. *Wow, this is high.* I keep my sight set on Jake and the dark abyss behind him. "Have you ever seen the movie *Fear*? The one with Reese Witherspoon and Mark Wahlberg?"

He gives me a questioning expression. "They did a movie together?"

"Yeah." I laugh. "We were pretty young when it came out, but I remember seeing it on TV when I was in junior high. It was right when I was in those *impressionable* years with boys."

"I'm all ears when it comes to the impressionable years."

I kick his ankle. "Yes, and I'm about to tell you the first time I remember wanting to feel that rush with a boy."

He leans back in his seat and tilts his head with a smirk. "I'm listening."

I roll my eyes. "In the movie, Mark Wahlberg plays a bad boy."

"Before Hardy, was he your muse for the bad boys in your books?"

A sharp laugh escapes my lips. "No way. I've never written a bad boy like Wahlberg in that film. He was psychotic actually, but that's beside the point. There's this scene where they ride a roller coaster together."

Just then, the ride stops with a jolt, and the car rocks back and forth. We're dangling high in the air—way too high from the ground.

I grip the edge of my seat as I continue with a swallow, "So, Reese's character is this good girl who starts dating the bad boy, who her dad doesn't approve of."

"Sounds about right."

"Of course. But when they're on the roller coaster, they get a little close together, and some things start to happen."

"What kind of things?" His thighs widen, his teeth skimming his lower lip.

"While the ride is going up the track, he sticks his hand up her skirt and starts to finger her right there. He gives her a mind-blowing orgasm with the wind in her hair and the movement floating in her body. I remember thinking how fun that would be."

"That does sound fun. Have you ever tried it?" The deep baritone of his voice makes my chest tighten. He's staring at me, daring me to tell him more. To want more.

The ride starts to move again.

I lick my lips as I turn to stare out at the pier below with its bright lights and people scattered about as the ride swings by the people standing, waiting their turn, and starts its ascent back up.

When I don't answer, he leans all the way forward, and I find myself doing the same. Our mouths are close as he places a hand on my leg, moving upward until his thumb is rubbing the inside of my thigh ever so gently.

"Has that fantasy ever been fulfilled, Lacey?"

I shake my head. "I've never had an orgasm while on a roller coaster."

"What about a Ferris wheel?"

In the reflection of the glass walls, I see my cheeks redden, not with embarrassment, but with heat. I'm flush and so very tempted.

"Would you really touch me like that?"

"Would you want me to?" he asks, his hand inching higher.

I nod but don't say a word. His smile rises on the side as he slowly removes his hand and sits back, making my chest ache with desire.

"If Marky Mark was your ultimate bad boy, why don't you write him?"

"Because I like Richard Gere better," I state with a grin, holding my fingers up. "Two classics. *Pretty Woman* and *An Officer and a Gentleman*."

"Classics? Those movies are ancient. I'm intrigued though, so do tell."

"The scene in *Pretty Woman* where he climbs her fire escape and rescues her? It's the reason I love romantic heroes. I think all of mine have a little Gere in them."

"Good to know," he says with a slight grin.

"Sorry, that's how my mind works. I just think these random thoughts sometimes. Being on this ride reminded me of the movie and I tend to speak what I'm thinking which catches people off guard."

His mouth parts as his eyes darken. "Sometimes, I think random things too."

The ride twirls us up, over the top, and back down. My stomach flips for reasons I'm not sure of. I hold on to the edge of the seat, thinking I just lost my equilibrium since I was staring at Jake and not at the world around us.

"Like how I really want to kiss you right now."

"Why don't you?" I say, almost as a dare.

He shakes his head. "I can't figure you out, Lacey."

My heart sinks right before it slides up to my throat again as we climb back up to the top.

"For years now, you've been this gorgeous girl who lives next door, never giving me the slightest inclination that you wanted me. I know you don't need a relationship and you distrust men. And yet you come and ask me to go places with you. To kiss you."

"I can leave you alone."

"Fuck no. Don't do that."

"But you just said—"

"What I didn't get to say is that it's a good thing you're wearing jeans tonight or else I'd be tempted to slip a hand under your skirt and make your fantasy a reality."

I grip the seat, trying to steady my breath, which is very ragged all of a sudden.

He leans back as he adjusts his own pants. My eyes widen, and I'm not sure if I want to laugh or swoon or even breathe. My mouth waters as I stare at those soulful eyes.

And now, I wish I knew why I hadn't worn a damn dress.

CHAPTER FOURTEEN

The moon is large tonight, bright white and casting a glow over the street as we enter our building. We're pretty quiet as we make our way up the elevator and down the hall. The doors to our apartments are calling to us like a dare.

I don't want to be forward and assume he wants to come in or that he'll invite me into his place. He hasn't even tried to kiss me tonight, and it leaves me feeling confused.

"Lace," he starts as we reach my door.

I smile up at him, but his face is stoic. It makes my own fall as I wait for him to ask what is on his mind.

"The guy you dated when you moved to Chicago, the one who kept you from believing in real-life romance, do you still think about him?"

I'm startled by his question, and it must show because he adds, "I can't imagine why someone as spectacular as you, who writes about romance so beautifully, has denied it for herself for so long."

My gut instinct is to ignore his question. Play it off with a witty retort and ask him to come in. But that wouldn't appease him. Jake is a soulful creature, the kind of man who listens and amends the situation. Problem is, there's no fixing me or my past.

I inhale as I try to find the right words. There aren't any, so I just start speaking, "It's not just Michael. That's his name, by the way. We moved to Chicago together after college, and I tried to make it as a writer, but I couldn't sell my work to a publisher. He told me I was foolish for dreaming, that I wasn't very well rounded at my craft, and I needed to get a job using the degree I'd earned. So, I did. I went to work at a production company as a broadcast assistant. That's where I met my best friend, Charisse.

"She's the only good thing that came out of that job because, within a year, Michael left me for another woman, and I was so angry. Not with him, but with myself for letting a man dictate how I should live my life. I finally took the leap of faith and self-published a book that I had given up on two years prior when I couldn't find an agent to work with me. That book turned into another and then another until I was able to quit my job, and then I started writing the novel that hit the best sellers list. In that book, the hero was greater than any man, greater than Michael, and better than my father who had abandoned my mother when I was a little kid. He was superior to the jerk who had taken my virginity in high school and broken up with me the very next day.

Yeah, I don't have the best track record when it comes to men. It's not that I don't believe there are better ones out there. I just don't believe there are any for me."

I don't realize I'm crying until Jake lifts a knuckle and wipes a tear from my cheek. I turn away, embarrassed, but he pulls my face back to his.

"Not only are there good men out there, Lacey Rivers, but there is also a man who wants nothing more than to be the best one for you."

His words are like candy for my aching heart, yet I deny it, turning my cheek because I'm afraid. Not by what he's saying. No, I'm absolutely petrified by the way he makes me feel deep down.

I feel like he might be good.

Too good.

My heart just can't handle that kind of hope.

I close my eyes and smile slightly. "I had a really great time tonight, Jake. Just let me hold on to that. For one more night." Stepping back, away from his hold on my cheek and toward my door, I bid him good-bye. "Try not to knock too early tomorrow. I have a deadline."

He grins, but it seems sad. "You know I don't believe in your office hours."

I roll my eyes and open the door. "Night, Jake."

Closing my door behind me, I lean against it and sigh, wondering how I managed to ruin a perfect good-bye. We had a fantastic date, and up until ten minutes ago, I was convinced he was coming back to my place.

Then, I went and shared my past with him.

Way to ruin the mood, Lacey.

I never, ever share myself like that with anyone,

and there I was, shoveling my past from the grave and tossing it at his feet, burying him in it. No wonder I don't go out. There's a reason I'm only with fictional men. I can delete the words on the page. I can't delete my mouth.

No. Who am I kidding? I might not share myself that often, but I certainly won't delete my words. I'm not ashamed to be me. I just want to meet a man who isn't the kind of man my mother raised me to be cautious of, and what the men of my past led me to accept as normal.

I want a man who is honest and sweet. Someone who keeps his promises and isn't afraid to have the uncomfortable conversations. A man who will stick around.

A man like Jake.

I've been keeping him at arm's length, for fear that he's bad. He might not turn out to be the man for me, but if that happens, it's not because he's cruel or unjust. A man like Jake Moreau dates with the end in mind. He's looking for his forever, and I won't even give him a decent chance.

Does he want one?

He must. He's been so patient with me. A neighbor, a friend, a date. The man comes off as an enigma, but that's only because it's so hard to believe he is exactly what he appears to be.

A good man.

"What is wrong with me?" I say out loud as I run my hands through my hair.

I need to go next door and talk to him and ... say

what? For a woman who writes dramatic love scenes, I am certainly at a loss for what to say.

I'm chewing on my thumb and wondering what to do when I hear a clicking sound.

No, it's a tapping sound.

Tap, tap, tap.

I rush over to the source of the sound that's coming from my living room and turn toward the window, where it sounds like a small object was thrown. I look out and down to the street three flights below. Jake is standing on the sidewalk, staring up at me. I open the window and stick my head out.

"Did you lock yourself out?" I call down to him.

"Go to your bedroom."

He walks away, and I close my window, utterly confused. Like a good girl, I follow his instructions and run over to my bedroom and open that window. There's a fire escape back here, so I climb onto it and search for him.

Jake is on the ground, jumping up to the ladder on the bottom of the second-floor fire escape and pulling it down. The sound of metal sliding across metal screeches in the night. In the same clothes from our trip to the Pier, he climbs up the ladder to the second-floor landing and then climbs the steep incline of the staircase that leads to mine. When he gets up here, I step back to the railing of my landing and look back at him.

His skin is flush, his chest is heaving like he ran a marathon, and his gaze is absolutely searing.

"What are you doing?" I ask despite my own racing

heart. I'm pretty damn excited to see him standing out here even though I'm confused as to why.

"I think I'm supposed to make a speech about rescuing you or you rescuing me or something like that." His lips tilt up in a smirk.

I narrow my eyes at his comment until I realize exactly what he's talking about. He's reenacting the final scene in *Pretty Woman*.

The smile wipes away from my face.

I'm not mad, nor am I upset. No, my lack of a smile is because I'm so touched, shocked, and beyond speechless.

Jake wasn't climbing up here on a whim.

He's here on a mission.

" 'So, what happens after he climbs up and rescues her?' " I recite the line from the film.

Jake grins that damn gorgeous smile that makes me weak in the knees. "Well? What is it?" His chest is still heaving, but it's not from exertion. He's staring at me in anticipation. In want and need and lust.

He's here to save me.

I take a step forward and place a hand on his chest. His head rises with a quick inhale at my touch.

His heart pounds wildly against my palm as I lean closer and say, " 'She rescues him right back.' "

I rise on my toes and kiss him in that slow, deep way that awakens every dormant, lust-filled cell in my body. His hands grip my waist and pull me in as his tongue glides along mine, stroking me tenderly.

Through his jeans, I can feel the hard length of him, so I lift my arms around his neck and push myself against him, wanting every inch. His mouth moves down my neck and up to my earlobe, biting lightly as I grip his shirt while tingles run down to my core.

I lift my head, and he claims the kiss again, hungrier than before.

His hand fists my hair as I run mine up the back of his shirt, anxious to touch his skin. We struggle as we move toward the window and have to break apart to crawl inside. I go first and watch as he bends his large frame through the open window and stands before me in the dark. The kitchen light is the only one on in the apartment, and its faint glow casts a heavenly brightness on his face.

His sharp jaw, smooth skin, and that perfect angle of his face in the shadows, plus those sinful chocolate eyes melt the clothes right off of me.

I lift my sweater and remove it, dropping it to the ground. Next, my jeans are unbuttoned. He steps forward and has his hands on my cheek and in my hair, pulling me close. His mouth crashes into mine. Kissing and loving on me, he lifts me in his arms and walks me to the bed.

I'm lying down, propped on my elbows as I watch him remove his henley. His ripped chest is on display. It's even better than when I got to paint it and when he was wearing that damn seafoam-green towel. This time, I get to touch it however I want.

So, I do.

Placing my palms on his pecs, I glide my fingers over his skin and let my thumbs graze his nipples. He sighs at the feeling of my hands on him and leans down to climb onto the bed, joining me.

"You know, if you wanted to get me in bed, you

159

could have just come in through the front door," I tease, continuing my exploration,

He stops his kisses and looks down at me. "Lace, I didn't do that to get you in bed. I climbed up here to show you that you're worth more than three bad memories. You deserve to be romanced. I want to show you what a real man can be."

"And what's that?" I ask breathlessly.

"Yours."

He takes his time in savoring my body. Starting at my clavicle, his tongue caresses my skin, moving down my chest, my stomach, and along the edge of my panties, eliciting a hiss through my teeth.

"Tell me if I'm going too fast," he says.

"Not fast enough," I respond impatiently.

He moves his head between my legs and kisses my core first on the outside of my underwear, making me squirm in anticipation. Then, he removes them from my legs, flinging them to the floor before placing his mouth and tongue over my throbbing clit.

"Jake," I gasp as he flicks the bud and runs his fingers up and down the inside of my thighs.

The sight is pretty damn spectacular as he kneels before me, lapping up my sex and gazing up at me with a loving expression, asking if I'm okay with what he's doing.

I nod, looking him square in the eye as my orgasm swarms low in my core. He's soft and gentle yet rough and dangerous. Even his shoulders are beautiful, and they flex as he wraps his arms around my thighs and pulls my core closer to his mouth. He's sucking on my clit and then pushing his tongue inside of me. When he licks me with long motions, I clench my duvet and grab hold for dear life as the orgasm builds inside me.

My head falls back as my back arches.

"Oh God," I cry.

He growls against me and sucks harder before gently licking with his tongue, causing my body to tremble from the inside out. Ripples of pleasure throb between my legs. I yank on Jake's hair as intense waves of ecstasy hit me hard. I cry out again and again, chanting his name as I fall back to the bed.

Tears well up in my eyes as I'm overcome with the heady emotion of my first orgasm by someone other than me in years.

As he works his way up my body, he takes in my face. "Hey there, Lacey girl. I told you, if it's too soon, we can wait." He lovingly strokes my hair as he looks down at me in concern.

I smile. "It's not that. I'm happy actually. And it scares me."

His shoulders fall in relief. "I have a secret," he says, and I'm all ears. "I'm scared too. I'm crazy about you. Maddeningly addicted. I'm laying a lot on the line too. I'm falling for a girl who doesn't believe in love."

Maybe it's because he's so damn good-looking or because he climbed my fire escape. Hell, it could be because I just had an intense orgasm, but in this moment, something about Jake has me lowering the barriers that protect my heart, and I'm completely honest with him.

"I'm crazy about you too."

"Really?"

I nod and feel for the buckle of his pants. "Delirious

and wild. I want all of you. Right now."

He doesn't waste any time. He takes a condom out of his wallet and tosses it onto the bed. His pants are discarded and pushed onto the floor. His boxer briefs are next. As he settles on me, his cock hits me inside, and the sheer proximity of it has me reeling in anticipation.

I reach down and grasp it in my hand. It's hot and heavy as I slide over the hardened shaft.

His forehead falls to mine. "Fuck, that feels so good."

"I need you inside me." My voice is desperate as I lift the condom and take it out of the wrapper.

He sits up on his knees, and from this angle, his cock looks massive. As I slide the rubber on his erection, I get excited at how incredible it will feel once it's inside of me.

"I'll go slow," he says as he settles between my legs.

"Don't you dare."

My words are rewarded with a kiss as he slides himself inside my core, and I gasp at the foreign feel of it. It's thick and hot, and already, my eyes roll to the back of my head as he thrusts his hips against my body.

My hips and legs are practically vibrating as he slides in and out. He leans down to take a sensitive nipple in between his lips and then lifts up to claim my mouth. His jaw is tight as he fights the urge to come, and I give him his out.

"Come, baby. Let it go."

"No." He shakes his head. "This is for you."

He raises one of my legs and pushes in further. The sensation is incredible, and coupled with his dedication to making me come, I'm in a lust-filled haze, writhing and panting beneath him. He pins his hips to hit the spot that seems to make me see double and slams into it relentlessly.

Our eyes lock as we surge past every barrier I have up. Beyond my past, crashing into my present. I come with a cry in the dark, clenching around him. His weight falls on me as he pumps into me like a machine, chasing his own orgasm as he grips me, kisses me, claims me, and absolutely owns me.

When he comes, it's with my name on his lips.

His hands are on my hips, and his mouth finds mine again.

I wrap my legs around him, and we fall to the side, kissing, gasping, and grasping on to one another like teenagers in heat.

I don't know what this man will do to my heart, but for tonight, I'm going to let him own it because being his is more than amazing.

CHAPTER FIFTEEN

I wake to the sun shining through the window and the heat of a warm body. My first reaction is to flinch before I remember who's lying next to me.

Staring at his back, I admire the pristine form of it. Broad shoulders. Tapered waist. He has a birthmark on his spine and another at the top of his ass. I run a finger from one to the next, connecting the dots and watching as his body shifts with the touch.

"Hmm," he hums as he rolls onto his back, pulling me into his arms and resting my head on his chest. "Good morning." When he kisses the back of my head, chills run through my body. "You don't like to snuggle, do you?"

I place my hand on his. "I'm used to having my own bed."

His chest rumbles with his laugh. "I'm aware. I tried to snuggle you last night, and you kicked me. I was tempted to build a pillow fort around me to avoid getting bruised."

I lean up and bite my lip. "Sorry. Was I really *that* bad?"

He pulls me in closer, snaking both his hands around me and wrapping a leg over my thigh. "I'm okay if you need your space to sleep so long as you let me do this to you when you're awake. Cuddle time is definitely a priority."

"Did you really just say 'cuddle time'?

"For the record, most women would love a man as affectionate as me."

"Leave it to you to find the one girl who needs her space," I say. When I feel him pulling away, I grip his back and push my body into him, letting him know I like him exactly where he is. "That said, I really like you invading my space."

His mouth leans down to my ear and neck, showing me just how appreciative he is for this physical connection.

I lean up to look at the clock, noticing it's almost eight. It's early for me, but I remember him saying something about having to be up at six for work. I guess that's what we get for staying up way later than we should have, but after we had sex, we sat and talked for hours before having sex again. It was the best night I'd had in a long time, and the sex was the cherry on top.

"Are you going to be late?" I ask, concerned.

"My mom will understand."

I look up at him in shock. "You are not going to tell your mom we slept together."

He chuckles as he grabs his cell phone off the nightstand and starts texting. "Fine. I won't tell her *that* or that we stayed up for hours, talking in bed before going for round two." He winks at me. "How about I tell her we went on an amazing date last night and that I took you to breakfast? She won't suspect anything since you live next door."

"Okay, that works better," I say, watching him punch in a message to Bobbi. "I'm surprised you're willing to lie to her about breakfast."

"I'm not lying. I still plan on feeding you. I make spectacular French toast." He puts the cell phone down, comes up behind me and grabs my waist, pulling me into him.

"Or we can skip breakfast and use the time for something even better?" I wiggle my ass against him and love the sound he growls into my ear.

"You're making it hard to leave this bed. How about you come to the flower shop with me today?"

I still. "You want me to come to work with you?"

"Yeah, it will be fun. I'll teach you all the dirty little secrets of the flower business."

A grin spreads across my face at the idea of spending the day with him. "I'm sure there's a real dark web of the petal pushers."

"You teasing me, Rivers?" He tickles my sides, and I laugh into him, only subsiding when he starts kissing my neck again as I run my hands down his torso.

"I have a confession to make. Rivers is a pen name."

With a bent arm, he holds his head up as he lies on his side and asks, "What's your real name?"

NAUGHTY NEIGHBOR

"Lacey Camille Wampo. I didn't think Wampo was romantic enough for a writer, and Rivers sounded so beautiful. And if I'm being completely honest, I kinda like having my own name. Something that's not associated with my father or my mother or anyone for that matter. I'm my own person. That must sound crazy to someone like you with strong family ties."

"No." He shakes his head slightly as he looks down with pursed lips. "It would be rude of me to assume anything about your feelings. I didn't have your upbringing. You must think I'm crazy for giving up my dream to fulfill a family obligation."

"Not at all. It's admirable. That's quite possibly my favorite thing about you. Which is why I would love to go to work with you today. You sure your parents won't mind?"

"Nah, they'd love to have you. My mom hasn't stopped talking about you since she met you the other day. You could bring your laptop, and if things get busy, you can sit in the back and write, so you'll still get your words in."

"Look at you, speaking author lingo."

"I pay attention to what you say." He moves a stray hair away from my face. "Sound good?"

"I think it sounds like the perfect way to spend the day."

I pull the covers off and hop out of bed, but he stops me short, reaching for me and sliding me underneath him.

"Okay, I was wrong. That was a good idea you had before."

I laugh out loud as his lips crash into mine, instantly making me lust for him and what his body can do to me.

"Lacey, I'm so glad you decided to spend the day with us. So, tell me, are you making one of your characters a florist? Perhaps a woman named Bobbi with age-defying beauty and business savvy, who takes the city by storm?"

Jake raises his brows. "You've read her books, Mom. The heroine falls in love."

"A woman in her fifties can have a love affair," she explains. Turning to me, she adds, "I'd like to fall in love with a firefighter who looks like Dylan McDermott."

"She's on a Tom Hardy kick right now," Jake says with a chuckle.

"Yes, but Tom Hardy is my dream love interest. I can definitely write a sexy and savvy floral designer from Chicago who gets rescued by a fireman with piercing blue eyes and thick, dark hair," I say with a smile, making him groan.

"What is up with the light eyes and dark hair?" he asks.

I laugh. "Even your mother agrees. It's the preferred heartthrob look."

Bobbi nods her head as she cuts the stem off a rose and places it in a vase.

Jake points his cutting shears in his mother's direction. "Don't let Pop hear you talk about lusting

169

about blue-eyed firefighters. And what does the fictional Bobbi do with the husband she has?"

"Write that he left her for a Sofía Vergara–type. It's your dad's celebrity hall pass, and it would make him happy to know he landed her in some alternate universe." She laughs at her joke as Jake bows his head, as if his parents were the ultimate embarrassment.

I giggle at their antics. "Noted. First, I have to finish my current book. The hero is an artist."

Jake lifts his head. "That was my idea, by the way."

I smile. "Yes, it was his idea. Maybe being here will bring some inspiration. I'm at a standstill in the story line, and I only have a short time to finish."

The front door to the shop opens, making a chime ring. A gentleman with dark blond hair, a smattering of gray on the sides, enters, carrying a box. He walks over to the counter, where Jake and Bobbi are making arrangements for the afternoon deliveries.

"My darling, these look beautiful." He gives Bobbi a kiss on the cheek as he looks at me with a grin. "Who is this young lady?"

Jake puts a hand on the small of my back. "Pa, this is Lacey."

I step forward, holding out my hand. "It's nice to meet you, Mr. Moreau."

"Please, call me Louis. Jake was right. You are even more beautiful in person than the photo on your author website."

My eyes are wide as I roll my head in Jake's direction. "Why are you showing my picture to your family?"

Louis saves his son. "I wanted to know more about the woman who has the ladies in my family going crazy as they keep their nose in a book. Bobbi wouldn't sleep; she was reading all night. And my Penelope has been going on and on about Jake's new friend who writes novels. And this one"—he points to Jake—"only has the kindest things to say about you."

That's so sweet to hear, especially since I've been pretty short with Jake in the past.

"He's been nothing but chivalrous, and he is very easy to spend time with."

Louis motions his hand in the air. "That's my son. He can make friends with a house fly. That's how we get so much business. He talks to everyone who comes in. His mother's son, that one."

I smile big at Jake as he finishes filling the vase in front of him.

"Lacey's going to hang out with us today," he tells his father. "Do you think you can stop with the flirting? You're a married man after all."

"Oh, hush. I do no such thing. Now, if she were Sofía Vergara, it would be a different story."

"Told you!" Bobbi says and starts laughing.

Louis looks back to me. "I'm glad you're spending the day with us. If you need anything, just let me know. This guy here hasn't quite mastered the needs of women yet." He thumbs over to Jake, who clutches his heart.

"Ouch. That hurts," he fakes. "Just because I'm not married doesn't mean I don't know how to please a woman."

I elbow Jake's stomach, and he laughs in response. Bobbi throws her hands up in the air, as if not claiming responsibility for anything that comes out of her son's mouth, as Louis shakes his head and turns toward the back room. I hear his laugh as he walks back there, followed by Bobbi.

I narrow my eyes at Jake, who just leans down, gives me a chaste kiss, and then follows his parents to the back, carrying two of the centerpieces.

As I chuckle under my breath, I take a seat on a stool at the table. Jake is back minutes later with a rag and wipes the counter down before sweeping up the floor. The table has four stools and there are photo albums on a nearby shelf. I pull one out and open it, marveling at the amazing centerpieces inside. This must be where newlyweds sit and look up inspiration for their weddings. It's a nice flex space and a good place for me to hang out while I'm a wallflower at the florist.

The day goes by smoothly. Louis and Bobbi go back and forth, making arrangements and getting them out for deliveries. Jake handles most of the front-end business—taking orders, making mixed bouquets, and checking out customers.

A man enters in the afternoon, looking for a bouquet for a girl he's dating. He doesn't want roses because he doesn't want to come off as too forward, but he doesn't want to give carnations because then she'll think he's cheap. He asks for Jake's opinion because, in his words, he's "friggin' clueless."

I never thought about how guys might prefer asking another man's opinion on something like flowers. Jake walks him over to the refrigerator, pointing to bins inside the cooler. I watch the man's face morph from apprehensive to relieved as Jake explains the flowers and gives him all of the options.

The end product is a gorgeous bouquet of a half-dozen red roses, purple hyacinths, and white lilies. If I were to receive them, I'd look at the flowers and see the romance in the red roses yet sense the connotation of a budding friendship and the pureness of a new relationship. The mixture elicits the right emotions for a new couple.

After the man pays, Jake turns to me, seeing the huge grin on my face. "What?" he asks, stepping closer to me.

"That was perfect, what you did there."

"You mean, how I did my job?"

"Yeah. It's impressive. You could have just tossed some baby's breath over roses and told him to have a good date. But you listened and worked with him. Plus, I'm pretty sure he wants to be your new best friend."

"I have that effect on people."

I teasingly punch him in the arm. "So cocky."

He leans down, briefly kissing my lips. "Only for you."

"I knew it!" I hear Bobbi say as she walks in from the back room.

I close my eyes, embarrassed.

Jake stands straight and speaks to his mother, "You know we're seeing each other? Hence the *I'm coming in late because I'm taking Lacey to breakfast this morning* text I sent you."

"I knew you were dating. I didn't know you were … *this*."

"And what is *this*?" he asks her with a tilted chin and matching grin.

"This is … this." With the flick of her finger, she looks at us like she has the best idea in the universe. "Lacey, you should come to the cottage with us. My daughters are dying to meet you!"

"Um, I …" I open my eyes wide to Jake, not sure if he would even want me there, let alone know if I even feel comfortable with going to a home with people I barely know.

He grins from ear to ear. "That would be fun. Everyone's going. You should come."

"Really?" I swallow. "Who's everyone?"

Bobbi smiles. "Us, Jake, his sister Milène and her husband. Penelope will be there too."

"Who watches the shop?" I ask.

"Louis comes back and forth. We're only open from eight to four, and the cabin is only an hour away," she explains.

"I'm taking two days off to spend time on the lake, and then I'll relieve Pa, so he can get some rest," Jake adds. "You mentioned you liked small towns and beautiful scenery. This has it all. You can work from the deck, and there's a hot tub."

"You had me at hot tub!" I say in a joking way when, really, I'm kind of excited Jake wants me to go. A little nervous about being around his sisters for the first time but happy. I rub my lips together and raise my shoulders. "I guess I'm going to the cottage."

Bobbi does a tiny bounce in celebration. "Yay! This is going to be so much fun. I'm going to call your sisters."

She runs off, and Jake steps in between my legs, sliding his hands onto my cheeks and lifting my head to face his.

"Are you just saying yes to be nice?"

"You should know by now that I'm not *that* nice," I tease.

"Sure you are. It's just behind the hard shell you keep up to hide how soft you are inside." He runs a thumb over my lips, and I kiss the pad of it. "You sure you're down to spend the weekend with me?"

I laugh. "I should be asking you the same thing. Don't feel like you have to bring me if you don't want to. I know you didn't really invite me."

He lowers his hands to the counter, placing one on each side as he pins me with his body and his stare. "Lacey?"

"Yes, Jake?"

"I'm not inviting you to the cottage."

"You're not?"

"No. I'm telling you to go. So, pack a bag. We're going to the lake." He kisses me, deep and soulful, making me whimper lightly. "And if you have any lingerie, I suggest you bring it."

"And if I don't?"

"Then, naked will do just fine."

He kisses me again and pulls away as the front door chimes, and a customer walks in.

My heart pounds for so many reasons, yet here we go. I guess I'm going away for the weekend with Jake and his family. Ideas pop in my head, and I get so excited that I grab my backpack, open my laptop, and start typing as fast as my fingers will allow me.

CHAPTER SIXTEEN

An hour outside Chicago, in the state of Wisconsin, is the resort city of Lake Geneva.

After leaving the flower shop, Jake and I went home and packed weekend bags, getting back into the car when it was already dark out. I might not be able to see much of the town on the drive, but the Gilded Age mansions are illuminated at night, showing the old-world charm of the beach town.

I should be nervous, but as we head up the long, circular drive, I find myself more in awe at the Victorian home in front of me than anything else.

"You said we were going to a cottage." My jaw is slack as I stare up at the three-story mansion with a four-car garage and, if I'm correct, a lakefront view.

"Yeah, the term is a bit deceiving. It's our family home outside of the city."

"Well, this certainly makes an impression."

He quirks a brow. "Are you saying you're now only interested in me for my family's money?"

I nod my head as I continue to stare at the shaker-style shingles and bright white molding around the windows. "You're lucky you have a big dick because that's the only thing more impressive than this house."

He blanches for a second as I step out of the car. "Wait. You can't drop the 'big dick' comment and then just walk out like that!"

With a laugh, I head to the back of the car to get my bag. "You bring girls here a lot?"

"I have, but I usually wait until we're a few months in. I wouldn't want her more impressed with the house than my cock," he teases.

I shake my head and kiss him on the lips. "Just so you know, you have nothing to worry about with me. You had me at the seafoam-green towel. Everything after that is gravy."

I walk toward the front door and hear him cheer behind me, "I knew it!"

We walk into the cottage together. The inside is equally as impressive as the outside with a two-story entry with floor-to-ceiling wainscoting and a large living room ahead with wall-to-wall windows overlooking a patio that's filled with people.

"She's here!" a girl's voice calls out from the patio.

Two girls, about my age, walk toward us.

"You have no idea how excited we are to finally meet you," one says.

"Yes, we were starting to think this guy was pulling our leg and you didn't really live next door to him," the other adds.

"Lacey, these are my sisters, Tweedledee and Tweedledum," Jake says with a smirk.

They slap his arms as they hug him from either side.

"Good to see you too, bro," a woman with long light-blonde hair and porcelain skin says to him and then leans into me for a hug. "I'm Milène."

"And I'm Penelope." The other sister with shorter, curlier hair bounces to me. "Come on in. We have a bottle of wine open with your name on it."

I smile at Jake as he winks and then heads into the kitchen, where his mom is preparing food.

The deck in the back of the house sits right over the lake, and with the sun going down, it's the most surreal setting of both beauty and nature.

They walk me to the side where a U-shaped couch is set up with a table that has a firepit in the middle. We all take a seat as Penelope pours me a drink, handing it to me.

"So, when did you first start writing?" Milène asks.

An instant smile graces my face. It's rare to meet people who want to talk about my writing unless I'm at a signing event. Finding people who love books, especially romance, as much as I do is a treat any day.

"It was something I dabbled in for a while before I finished my first one. Then, I sat on it for two years before I actually published it."

"Why?" they both ask in unison.

"It's a long story."

Michael's disdain of my writing was cold and callous; his impact on me left a scar. And yet, for the first time, I don't have this urge to pretend like that part of my life didn't exist.

"I let a man convince me I wasn't good enough."

"That's horrible," Milène says.

Penelope's mouth opens like she's catching flies. "What a jerk."

I agree, "Not all men are willing to let their woman dream."

My eyes roam to Jake who came back outside, and the words of encouragement he's given me from the moment he found out I was an author come flooding through me. He's never faltered in his praise for me, even before he knew I was good at it.

"Those men are assholes." Jake is serious with his statement as he joins us.

My mouth lifts to the side, as does my heart. "It's rare a man has the instinct for making women feel appreciated."

Milène's eyes sparkle as she looks back and forth between Jake and me. She nudges me in the side. "Well, we're sure happy you didn't listen to that jerk."

"We love reading your stories," Penelope adds as she raises her glass to cheers me. "Although I might have a hard time with reading the sex scenes in any future books. I might start picturing you and my brother." She makes a face that has me giggling.

"That's my cue to leave." Jake places his hand on my shoulder and brushes the hair to the side before rubbing his thumb and forefinger on my earlobe.

I watch him walk inside the house. When I turn back to the girls, Milène nudges Penelope's leg with a huge grin on her face.

"Okay, that was pretty cute," Penelope says.

"Beyond adorable." Milène points to me. "Just don't go putting it in one of your books, so I don't think of my brother when I'm envisioning your hero."

Little do they know, their brother is the only inspiration I have these days. Without him, I'm at a loss for words. I should tell him he's my muse. I know he'll love it. However, if I do, I might break the magic. He'll stop being himself, and I won't be able to play the heroine anymore. This fantasy might end, and … well, that's the scary part.

I don't want anything to end.

Louis and Bobbi come outside, and I say hello to them for the second time today. A guy with reddish hair and a goatee follows them and takes a seat by Milène. He introduces himself as her husband, Wayne. It reminds me of when Jake stood up for my books to my mother, talking about his sister and her relationship with her husband and how my stories helped her escape the reality of work and chores, bringing her back to what it was like when they first met. I wonder what their story is.

I start small and ask how they met.

"In a plumbing supply store!" she exclaims like it's the craziest place in the world. "I was working on a residential property, and he was the lead contractor. Our client asked us to meet them to discuss textiles for the house. We got there on time, but the client was late," Milène explains.

Wayne lovingly looks at her. "I knew she was the woman I was going to marry as soon as she walked in, wearing those four-inch heels," he says with a grin. "It took her a few dates, but I convinced her."

"He offered to remodel my bathroom at cost. I was going to give it ten dates or until my new claw-foot tub was in." Her joke earns her a noogie from her husband.

I laugh. "How did the bathroom come out?"

She sighs. "Five years later, and I'm still waiting for it to be done."

Wayne laughs. "Five years, two kids. We've been busy."

The easy camaraderie that comes off between the two as they joke about their marriage and one another is endearing. Either it's a show or these two really are in love.

Penelope is looking at them wistfully. "Someday, I'll get to where they are. I'm still waiting for my Mr. Right. Now, Lacey, if you can just tell me where I can meet a man, you'll be more than my favorite author. I'll be your best friend."

I let out a loud laugh. "Well, you could start by knocking on your neighbor's door."

Both girls grin as they glance each other's way.

"Chicken's on the grill," Louis announces. "Does everyone have a drink, or can I get anything?"

Jake walks through the back door with two drinks in his hands. "Dad, take a load off. I'll finish everything."

Louis brushes him off. "You go sit with your girl. Besides, I can tell by the holes in your pants that you've already been working too hard."

Looking down at his charcoal jeans, Jake explains, "They're stylish."

Louis points his utensil at them. "They cost too much to have holes in them."

With a shake of his head, Jake laughs. "That's the point!"

He heads toward his mom, who's standing at the outdoor dining table, and grabs the plates from her hands.

There's a sweet nature to Jake. He's both caring and helpful. I've always seen him as this player from next door. Knowing now how charismatic he is in any situation paints him in a different light.

We all casually hang out while we wait for dinner to be ready. Wayne blends in as if he'd been around them his whole life. If I were to see them for the first time and someone asked me who I thought was family and who I thought had married in, I wouldn't be able to tell.

They all talk and laugh like they've known each other their entire lives, and Louis acts the same with his son-in-law as he does his daughters. When I see him tease Wayne for his new haircut, I'm both shocked and happy that he doesn't take offense or think it's weird. He treats Louis just like he would his own father by cracking a joke about him going bald.

I guess I'm surprised because I've never had family like this. I have no siblings, no dad, and my aunts and uncles or grandparents live far away, so I only see them on occasion. Just saying people are your family doesn't make them the true definition. Charisse and Melody are more my family than my blood relatives are.

Milène is telling everyone a story of how she stood up to her daughter's teacher the other day when I hear Penelope yell out, "Liar, liar, chickallo dire. There's no way you said that to her."

Milène holds her arms up in defense. "I swear. I was so mad."

I look at Penelope, trying to hold back my laugh. "What did you just say to her?"

Penelope and Milène burst out laughing as Wayne fills me in, "You'll learn they have a lot of, what they call, 'Jakeisms,' " he says, holding up his fingers as quotation marks.

"Jakeisms?" I ask, confused.

"Yes, there are tons of them," Wayne says. "I never hear him say them, but they bring it up all the time."

"So, when Jake was younger, he thought he knew all the lyrics to songs and things that people would say. Only he didn't. He used to watch this show where they would say, 'Liar, liar, pants on fire.' So, one day, something was happening, and Jake busted out with, 'Liar, liar, chickallo dire,' " Milène says.

"But those aren't real words." I squint my eyes, trying to figure out his logic.

"Exactly! That's why we still say it to this day. He for sure thought that was what the kids on TV were saying."

Milène covers her mouth like she's been caught saying something she shouldn't have. When I follow her gaze, I see Jake coming back to join us with a smirk, shaking his head.

"Are you guys seriously telling her about *liar, liar, chickallo dire*?" he asks.

Everyone laughs.

"Hey, we were just having a conversation, and I called Milène out. It was Wayne here who said it was a Jakeism." Penelope states matter-of-factly.

"Way to throw me under the bus," Wayne teases.

"So, what other Jakeisms are there?" I ask.

"No!" Jake says quickly, pointing to everyone but trying to hold back his grin.

Milène scoots over to me, whispering in my ear, "Don't worry. You'll learn a few more by the time the night's over. Just pay attention."

"Will you get away from her?" Jake shoos her away. "Dinner's ready, so come on. Chow's on."

I turn to Milène, wondering if that's one, and she grins.

"Nope, that's my dad's saying," she says as she wraps her arm through his in a loving manner.

As we all sit around the table, story after story of good times the family has shared float around.

I learn that Jake was a theater kid growing up. He loved set design and even won an award from the state.

I turn to him. "I didn't know you did theater."

He shrugs. "I had a minor role. My passion was behind the scenes."

"He only signed up as a way to pick up girls," Milène teases.

"Hey now, not in front of Lacey." He fills my water cup with a nearby pitcher.

"Like I didn't already know that aspect of you," I say with a deadpan expression.

Wayne leans in, abruptly changing the subject and looks at Jake and me with a seriousness written all over his face. "Okay, here it is. The make-or-break question of the day."

I raise my brow to Jake in confusion.

He seems to know where this is going because he just looks down with a grin as Wayne holds his two hands up and asks rather cautiously, "White Sox or Cubs?"

"Huh?" is all I can say.

Penelope rolls her eyes. "Boys are dumb."

"Be careful how you answer this one. It could be the beginning or the end of a beautiful evening," Bobbi adds jokingly, yet her tone says otherwise.

My eyes widen as I wonder if she's being serious. Jake shrugs, letting me know his family takes their Chicago sports very serious.

"I'm not a sports enthusiast. That's no news flash," I state. "However, growing up as the only granddaughter of my late grandfather, I had the responsibility of sitting with him and listening to him share his baseball knowledge. Of those years, I firmly remember three things." I hold up my fingers to tick each item off. "Ernie Banks is the best infielder of all time. Wrigley Field is the cathedral of baseball. And you should never, ever root for a team with footwear as a mascot. I'll always root for Chicago, but the Cubs are my team."

Jake grins, and Wayne lets out an audible sigh.

"She can stay," he says as Jake puts his arm around me.

"I had every intention of it. Now, if she'd said White Sox, we would have had to conduct a lobotomy first!" Jake's joke gets everyone laughing, and we go back to our banter and fun.

After dinner, we sit around a firepit in the backyard, drinking wine and talking some more. Bobbi brings out s'mores ingredients, and I show Jake how to roast the perfect marshmallow. He likes them burned, which is so gross. I take my time, browning the perfect mallow to get a golden coat.

Around eleven o'clock, everyone turns to their rooms. I help Jake straighten up the back deck, and we finish our drinks as we wait for the fire to die down.

He lifts my hand to his mouth and kisses my knuckles. "How about we get in the hot tub?"

The idea of being alone with him fills me with warmth and desire. "Okay," I whisper right before he kisses my lips.

"Go get your swimsuit on, and I'll meet you back out here."

"I don't know where my room is."

He chuckles. "You can take my room. Up the stairs, second door on the right."

"You're not going to show me up like a gentleman?"

"Trust me when I say, what I have planned is not gentlemanly."

His grin makes my chest tighten and my breath hitch.

"Now, go get dressed." He slaps my ass, and I yelp in response.

CHAPTER SEVENTEEN

I walk up the staircase and follow his instructions to find his room—navy-blue walls, distressed wood furniture, and a massive king-size bed. My duffel bag is lying on top of the duvet, which makes me smile. I didn't even know he'd walked it up here.

After I get my swimsuit on, I grab a robe from the back of the bathroom door and quietly make my way through the house so as not to wake anyone. It would have been wise to ask where the hot tub was, so I aimlessly wander to the back deck again in search of it. The air is thick with the scent of burned ash from the firepit. It's really chilly too. I rub my arms as I walk along the walkway to the side of the house, where I hear the sound of the tub's motor.

It's dark out here, except for two tiki torches lit on each side of the hot tub. Jake is already in with his clothes folded neatly on a nearby chair.

"Do you always bathe in the dark?" I ask, noting he left the other six tiki torches unlit.

"Only when I don't want anyone to see what I'm doing in here."

I quirk a brow. "And what is that?"

"Naked hot-tubbing. I hope you don't mind."

I shrug nonchalantly, playing with him. "I'll live."

He grins. "You look cute in my robe."

"Thanks. I thought you were more of a towel guy."

"I am. But my mother frowns on men walking around the house in a towel, so the robe wins. That said, I happen to think robes are entirely overrated."

I undo the belt. "Do you find them offensive?"

"Devastatingly. You need to discard it immediately."

Lowering it from my shoulders, I let it fall to the floor, revealing my two-piece bathing suit. A simple black bikini with strings that tie on the ends. "Better?"

"Much," he groans as his eyes rake over my body, staring at the triangles that cover my breasts, down my stomach, and at the sliver of fabric over my hips.

His tongue darts out of his mouth and skims his lower lip, like he's a starving man. A chill runs up my body, and it's not from the crisp autumn air.

"Aren't you going to join me?" he asks.

I walk to the tub and climb in. It's a large square with plenty of places to sit, so I take a seat on the other side of him, stretching out my toes to the seat beside him.

He pouts. "Do you always have to make things so hard on me?"

"I don't know. Do I?" My question is asked with every sexual innuendo in mind.

He gets the joke and laughs out loud.

I lean my head back as the jets push against my back, relieving the tension I didn't even know I was holding.

He wraps his hand around my foot and pulls it onto his leg, massaging the pad.

"A girl could get used to this," I sigh and close my eyes. With my hands floating on the water, I let the bubbles pop under my palms as I take in the peaceful feeling surrounding me. Nothing but the crickets in the background and the hum of the jets fill the air.

"What are you thinking about?" he asks.

"How peaceful this is," I respond without having to think.

"Yeah, I've always liked it out here."

"I meant, with you."

My admission has me popping my eyes open. It's my truth, yet saying it out loud makes me feel awkward and vulnerable.

I sit up a little, but he squeezes my foot, relaxing me.

"I'm happy when I'm with you too, Lace."

My face heats as I look at him. His hair is wet, slicked back with his fingers. His skin is glistening in the soft glow of the lights. He comes off as ethereal. A beautiful man massaging your feet in a hot tub is something women dream about. If I stare at him too long, I'll never want to wake up.

Leaning my head back, I stare up at the sky. It's a pitch-black night with every star illuminated.

"Wow," I breathe. "You don't get this in Chicago."

"The queen is out tonight," he says, making my eyes gaze over to him. "Cassiopeia. You can see it easily. Just find the Big Dipper—"

"I have no idea where that is."

Jake's jaw falls. "Baby, we have to get you a tutorial on the stars. Come here."

He motions with his finger for me to join him on his side of the tub. I swim-walk over, taking a seat beside him, and he swings an arm around my shoulder, pulling me in.

We lean back, and he takes my hand, lifting it up to the sky and using it as a pointer. "The Big Dipper rotates around the North Star. At any time of the year, you can use the Big Dipper to find Cassiopeia. They're like riders on opposite sides of a Ferris wheel."

"How so?"

"They're part of the spinning wheel of stars that move around the North Star. Cassiopeia rises up while the Big Dipper plunges down." He moves my hand to the place where the star formations are in the sky. "That *W*-shape is Cassiopeia."

"You know, there is something inherently romantic in the stars. I bet this queen was so beloved by her people to have been placed there."

"Um, no. Long story short, she was incredibly vain. Went to the seashore and told Poseidon, god of the sea, that she was more beautiful than his wife and all his daughters. Pissed him off. Then, she went to Hera, queen of the gods, and said the same thing to her. Hera grabbed some rope, tied Cassiopeia in her throne, and launched her so high in the sky that she got stuck upside down. Hera pretty much shouted, 'You think you're beautiful? Now, you can show the whole world for all of eternity!' And now, she does. Just upside down and tied to her chair."

I let out an awkward laugh. "That's horrible. I thought constellations and stories of the gods all had romantic meanings."

"This one still does." He taps my nose and looks back up at the sky. "Cassiopeia's husband was so grief-stricken when he heard about what had happened to her that he asked Zeus to send him to the sky with his wife. Like a good friend, Zeus did, flinging Cepheus right next to his wife." Jake points to the left of the *W*-shaped stars and says, "They're still clinging to each other. Cepheus kinda looks like a stick house that children draw."

"I see it!" I say way too loudly when I map out the stars he's talking about. I turn my head slightly, so I can see him. "You're really smart, Jake."

"I wouldn't say that. But when I like something, I study it well."

"What do you like? Other than stars and flowers, of course."

"What do I like?" He taps his chin, as if pensively thinking. "Good wine. A great book." He winks, and I roll my eyes. "Clothes. Now, I know my dad teases me about this, but I really do appreciate a finely made shirt. Music. I follow a lot of underground artists around the city. And most importantly"—he places his finger under my chin and tilts my head, so our lips align perfectly— "I like you."

"Does that mean you study me?"

"Daily."

His lips are warm as they place the softest of caresses against mine. My skin prickles with gooseflesh as his mouth lowers to my jaw and sucks lightly when he moves to the tender skin on the side of my neck.

"You're an introvert, but when you let someone into your world, you light up the darkest rooms." He stops kissing me and looks in my eyes, as if his words shouldn't be overlooked by his actions. "I mean that. You hide behind your computer, but when you step outside of your walls, you're witty and entertaining. You're bright, and I haven't had this much fun, just talking to a woman, in a long time." His tone is deep, and his face is serious.

My heart stills, as does my breath, at his very sweet words. It's not just what he said. It's how he said it. He stares into my eyes. I feel the heat of his gaze, and I know there are more words he wants to say, but he's holding back. Not because of his own insecurities, but because of mine.

"So, you like me for my brilliant mind," I joke pathetically.

He doesn't flinch. "Trust me, I want you for your gorgeous ass and tits, which are so damn hot, even when they're covered in an ugly-ass sweatshirt."

"They're not covered tonight. Well, not by much."

"Is that an invitation?" His eyes grow dark as his chest rises.

"It's a demand," I whisper centimeters from his mouth.

He lifts me by the waist and settles me onto his lap. His lips are hard against mine as his hands glide gently up my sides.

Our tongues dance as I wrap my arms around his neck, pushing my breasts on him and grinding myself against his naked form. Without a suit on, his cock flinches up with the contact, sliding against me with the thin material of my bathing suit feeling like it's going to burst at the seams.

He undoes the strings of my top, and it falls to the water, bouncing and floating in the bubbles. There's a shadow casting over his face so it's hard to tell, but there's one thing I can see clearly. Jake is happy.

"You're beautiful, Lace. I don't tell you that enough, but damn, every inch of you is drop-dead gorgeous."

"I bet you say that to all the girls."

"I might have, but I swear to God I never meant it as much as I do when I look at you."

His hands rise to each side of my face, caressing my cheeks and pulling me down for a kiss so passionate that I might combust right here. My breasts rub against his hot skin, and the feeling of us so close—and being so naughty—has me reeling in lust.

"Won't someone hear us?" I ask, remembering what it was like as a teenager sneaking around.

"Not if you're quiet." He dares me with his words and his actions as he sucks on my nipple, making me gasp as sensations ripple through me, down to my core.

I grip his hair and pull.

"I love it when you pull my hair." He smiles against my skin and then gives a nip. I reward him with another tug as I grind against him. "And when you rub like that over the tip of my cock, it feels like fucking heaven. Do it again."

I do as he requested, listening as he moans my name like I'm a damn queen needing praise.

His hands move down to my ass, squeezing it, and then they slide to the front, pushing my bottoms to the side. I lift up a little, giving him the perfect view of my breasts to nip and suck on as he runs his finger over my clit and rolls around. I arch my back and grip his shoulders, holding on tight. When his fingers slide down my folds and enter me, I steady myself as pure lust starts to take over.

As I roll my hips against his hand, virtually riding him, he tells me how wonderful I am, how he loves when I move my body like this, and how amazing I look against the stars in the sky. His words are like a waterfall, and I want to bathe in them as I chase my orgasm. His thumb rubs those vicious circles, and his fingers pump inside of me, eliciting heavy breaths and moans from me that need to be quieted by his kisses.

I've gone years without sex with a man, and now, I feel like a fiend, needing it so badly that I can't breathe.

"Jake." I close my eyes from every nerve on my body lighting on fire. I ride out my orgasm until he removes his hand and wraps it around my head, kissing me hard. "I need you inside of me."

He closes his eyes and mumbles under his breath, "Fuck."

"What?" I ask, grinding myself against him more.

"I can't believe I wasn't thinking about using a condom in here. Can we take this to the bedroom?"

I take a deep breath in, not wanting any of this to stop until he's made me come and I'm floating from the high. "I'm on the pill."

His eyes dart to mine as he runs a finger down my cheek. "Are you sure?"

I pull back to stare in his eyes. "That I'm on the pill? Yes, I'm positive," I joke, but I see the look in his eyes. He's asking about more than the physical pill. He needs to know if *I'm* okay with this. "You don't make a habit of this kind of thing though, right?"

He grins and leans up to kiss my lips once more. "You'll be my first."

My heart swells as I pull him in, kissing him harder, chasing the sensation we nearly lost.

As his hand moves to position himself at my entrance, I lift slightly before I slide down on his hardened shaft, feeling the fullness take over me. We both gasp at the intensity of the situation.

Holding each other tightly, we allow what we're doing to sink in, enjoying every minute, before I slide up and start to pulse.

The water moves around us as he grips my ass, guiding my movements and helping to lift me up. Feeling him fill me to the brim makes my head fall down to his shoulder.

"Oh God," I whisper into his ear as he slams into me once more.

He pulls back, so he can see my face, wanting to catch every word, every gasp that escapes from me as he moves my body with his, bringing me to heights I didn't know were possible.

Heights I've only ever written about.

Words fill my brain of how I would write this moment but nothing's fitting exactly what I'm feeling. Right here. How I would put to paper what he's doing to me and how my body's reacting. And that's when it hits me.

There are no words.

I could string together every adjective of how to explain the way his cock slides in and out of me, but none would let the world know just how amazing it actually is.

I'm going to try though. I'm going to try to shout it from the rooftops, letting my readers know that sex has been nothing until now. Until Jake. He's my muse, and I'm living the fantasy of being my own heroine.

He picks up his pace, and I have to bite my lip, gripping on to him for dear life so I don't scream out my release as I clench against him, letting the orgasm ripple through me while the water around us splashes.

His lips find mine again as his own release comes inside me. Listening to his gasps and gulps for air only makes the entire moment more special.

Knowing I'm doing to him the exact thing he's doing to me solidifies it.

For the first time in years, my life is better than fiction.

CHAPTER EIGHTEEN

"Zip-lining?"

"No."

"Paddleboarding?"

"Do I look like a guy who paddleboards?"

"Well, what do you have planned for today? I have twenty thousand words to write, so if you're keeping me off my laptop, it'd better be for a good reason." Like an insolent teenager, I'm standing with my hands on my hips, tapping my foot and waiting for him to tell me what the day's itinerary is.

Instead of stating it, he takes a seat in the chair near the window of his bedroom and puts his feet up on the window ledge as he grins. "Changed my mind. Surprise me."

My foot stops tapping. "Surprise *you*?"

"Yes. I'd love for you to plan the day for us."

Despite the cocky grin on his face, I know he's dead serious. His eyes twinkle, like he's daring me to take him up on this offer. Good thing I never let a man have power over me, so a dare is something I'll gladly take.

I grab my phone and fall onto the bed.

"Does this mean you give up?" he asks, sliding his feet off the windowsill.

I lift my head with a scowl. "Hell no. I'm gonna plan the best damn date in the history of dates. Now, go make yourself pretty because we have plans."

An hour later, we're in his car, and he's following directions to the address I put in the navigation system. He looks handsome in his jeans, camel-colored sweater, and brown leather sneakers. The aviator glasses on his face make him the epitome of cool, so I lean over and kiss him on the jaw. Liking the affection, he places a hand on my knee.

I'm pretty impressed with my own outfit I put together today. Skinny jeans—yes, I own a pair—and calf-height boots with a long sweater that falls off my shoulder a little. I have to wear a camisole underneath, and today's has a hint of lace. I blew my hair out and am wearing a touch more eye makeup. I'm not dressing up to please a man. I just happen to like the way his eyes light up when he sees me dolled up. It makes me feel good inside.

We reach the final destination, and Jake slides his glasses down his nose as he looks up. "You brought me to an orchard?"

"Perfect, I know. Autumn in the Midwest screams apples!"

"Actually, when I think of Wisconsin, I think of cheese."

"And apples are a perfect pairing. Now, let's go be super cute and pick some apples."

We grab a bucket and head to the path that leads toward the orchards, where we can pick our own apples. The views are breathtaking as we stroll the lanes of giant trees ripe with fruit. Parents are taking Instagram-worthy photos of their kids, and couples stroll while families argue over how many apples is too many.

Jake decides that since we have one bucket, we can only fill it with the world's best, crispiest apples. So, we make it a game. If someone sees a good one, we will stop at nothing to get it. I sit on his shoulders to reach a Red Delicious. He climbs a tree to get a Honeycrisp I'm certain is going to be juicy. I jump like a lunatic until I can reach an Empire.

We play hide-and-seek at the base of trees and then make out like teenagers behind the thick of leaves.

He takes a ton of selfies of us. My favorite is the one with his tongue in my ear while I'm making a crazy face. He likes the one where we're just looking at the camera, happy and content. It's actually my second favorite because he has a great smolder in that one.

There's a corn maze near the main barn, so we run through it, hand in hand, getting wildly disoriented and having no idea how to get out. Luckily, there's a seven-year-old who guides us to safety, and we laugh that we needed to be rescued by a child.

Inside the barn, they're having a cider tasting. Jake grabs three gallons along with an additional three bushels of apples and two pies.

"You're gonna eat all that?" I joke as he pushes his cart to the front to pay.

"This is all for my family back at the house. Everything, except for the apples we picked. Those are magical apples, and they're all ours."

"Now, if they had some spiked cider here, that would be magical," I joke, and the cashier points out the door.

"We have a hard-cider barn on the other side of the corn maze. You can do a tasting there."

Jake's teeth show with his grin. We place everything in the car and then walk into the hard-cider barn with our hands rubbing together, eager to try the good stuff.

There's a small bar at the end of the room, and Jake moseys over with his hand out to shake the gentleman's hand on the other side, reading the name on his shirt. "Fritz, you're just the man we want to see. My girl and I are on our fifth first date and would like to try some of your amazing cider. The more potent, the better." He winks, and I roll my eyes at his charm.

"Our *fifth* first date?"

He leans his elbow on the bar and explains, "The bar was our first date as friends. The Italian restaurant was our first date as TikTok kissers. The museum was our first date when I was trying to impress you, so we'd be more than friends. The third at Navy Pier was our first date when we," he leans in and whispers, "fucked afterward."

I hit him in the arm, but he doesn't seem to care as he points to the orchard.

"And this is our first date as us."

A slow, broad smile graces my face. "Us."

"Us." He kisses me and then turns back to Fritz. "Now, my man, you can't embarrass me with my girl on our fifth first date, so please, show us your finest variety."

Fritz seems enamored with Jake's wit. "So, you want the high alcohol content?"

With a point and a wink, he laughs. "You got it."

"Well, brother, let me give you the full-service treatment. I take it, neither of you has done a cider tasting before?" he asks, and we both shake our heads. "We have to get you guys the entire flight."

Fritz puts champagne glasses on the table and fills the first two. "Unlike wine, cider is made through various techniques and comes in a huge range of flavors. We'll start with the least interrupted ciders. This one is fermented from apples only."

I lift my glass and hold it up to Jake. "To the new champagne."

He clinks his glass with mine, and we drink them way too quickly.

"Damn, that's good," Jake says and motions toward the bottle. "I'll be taking a bottle of that."

As we drink our next glass of cider with spices, Fritz tells us—without oversimplifying the chemistry and steps involved—how ciders are made. Jake is fascinated by every word and asks a ton of questions.

Our next glass is barrel-aged cider. I love it so much that Jake tells Fritz we're taking a case.

We try pear cider and one with honey. Neither of us is a fan, but we still drink the entire glass. By the time we get to the brandy, Jake and Fritz are trading jabs

203

back and forth like they're longtime friends. He's not drunk. No, Jake is just personable like that. I know that anywhere I go with him, he'll see someone he knows or meet someone new. Everyone enjoys his company, and he seems to genuinely like people. I might not be as outgoing as he is, but boy, do I love watching him in action. His demeanor is so easygoing, and his spunk is spot-on.

And even though he's engrossed in conversation with someone else, he always has his hand on me.

We finish our flight and walk away with way too many bottles of cider. On the way home, we take the scenic route, listening to music and just enjoying the drive. His hand holds mine, tracing small circles on my palm. The lingering touch is soothing and sweet.

He hums along to the song on the radio, and I fall into the seat and sigh, completely distracted by the sunset ahead when something stirs inside me.

It's like a mini earthquake, where the floor falls from beneath my feet. I have to sit up and grip my chest. I look over at Jake, and he's just driving with a lazy smile on his face.

He turns to me and tilts his head. "You okay, babe?"

I nod, breathing harshly. I put a bright smile on my face even though my heart is pounding and my hands are clammy.

"Yeah. I think it was the cider. Too many bubbles," I lie because it's more like a panic attack.

He laughs and kisses my hand, looking back toward the winding road and enjoying the drive.

Meanwhile, I sit here, confused by this sensation. For a moment there, I thought I was dreaming.

Dreaming of a day where Jake and I were in love.

Dreaming of a forever.

Dreaming with our eyes wide open is dangerous. That's when people fall apart. It scares the hell out of me.

"Do you mind if we take a detour?" he asks.

I nod even though I thought we were already on one. As if sensing I'm having a moment of unease, he lifts my hand to his lips and places a kiss on the top, giving it a squeeze. His body tilts slightly toward me as he drives. It makes me curl my leg under me and face him fully.

He pulls up to a cliff overlooking the valley. It's vast and deep, beautiful with the orange glow of the early evening in the horizon. He lowers the windows in the car and opens his door. I do the same and get out, walking toward the edge.

The view is stunning, but I feel the heavy weight in my belly shift up to my heart. I take a deep breath of the sweet lake air.

Behind me, the music from his car is loud. A soulful melody plays, and he closes the door as he walks over to me.

"I'm going to do something super cheesy but ridiculously romantic," he says, taking my hands.

I look at him quizzically. "Are you warning me for a reason?"

"I'm preparing you." He pulls me close and wraps my hands around his neck. "To be utterly and tragically enraptured by me."

I laugh out loud. "I love when you get all cocky on me."

He kisses my nose. "I know."

I follow his lead as he sways from side to side. His hands tighten on my lower back as he holds me closely.

"What brought this on?" I ask as we dance in the breeze.

"I just had a feeling you needed an interlude."

He knows there's something off with me. It's comforting and frightening at the same time.

My body feels rigid, even as I mold myself against him. My chest rises as I take in a hard breath and lift my chin. That's when I see it. The look in his eyes.

Those deep brown eyes are staring at me with an intensity that holds me, wraps me in a warm blanket, and pulls me in closer. There's a crinkle in his eyes as he looks at me with a demeanor that has me letting go of that breath I was holding. I rest my forehead against his, breathing in his air, drinking in his expression, and staring back into those damn eyes that make me melt.

This is what he does to me.

He doesn't tear down my walls. No, he lets me keep them up. But he opens his own up and welcomes me and all of my issues into his world, holding on for dear life and letting me know he's with me.

And I fall hard through his walls and grip on to him, placing my head on his shoulder. I let this man—this beautiful, charismatic man—hold me as we dance on a cliff, keeping me from falling. Keeping me where my feet are planted firmly on the ground because that's where I need to be. And that's where he'll have me.

CHAPTER NINETEEN

I've been on a writing spree. Unlike the last sprints that came in spurts, I've spent the last five days writing like my life depends on it. From dawn to dusk, my fingers tip-tap on the keyboard. When I'm not creating new scenes, I'm editing and molding the previous ones, building out the story to be something big, bright, and beautiful. It's amazing how the words are coming to me so easily now. What started as the hardest book I'd ever written has ended as the easiest.

Once the sun sets, I close my laptop, and enjoy my second favorite pastime: Jake.

Knock, knock, knock.

Where his knock was once an inconvenience, it's now a welcome distraction from a hard day's work. Tonight, he's standing at the door in a pair of navy pants, a crisp white button-up, and that damn grin I've become addicted to.

It doesn't hurt he has a bottle of wine in his hand too.

I wrap my arms around him and pull him into my apartment with my lips on top of his.

"This is quite the greeting," he says.

"I finished today."

He yanks his head back. "Seriously? That's awesome. Looks like I should swap this baby out for a bottle of champagne."

"Not yet. I just sent the chapters to my agent, Wendy. I'm trying not to be nervous, but I can't help it. This book means a ton to my career. I also really love the story. It's my favorite I've ever written, and I'm afraid she'll tell me to edit something or that she doesn't like the ending, but I really don't want to change a thing. Where normally I'm up to people's suggestions, this one I want to leave just as I originally wrote it."

"I'm sure it's brilliant."

He leans down and kisses me again, taking it deeper than our first one. The bottle somehow finds its way to the counter because, now, his hands are on my ass, lifting me up so I can wrap my legs around his waist. As he walks me back to my room, I unbutton his shirt and look forward to some naked celebration time.

I'm sprawled out on the bed, my knees parted, as he settles himself between me and does that hips-rocking thing that drives me wild. My kisses are desperate, but he pulls away and stares down at me. There's a twinkle in his eye, and his mouth is upturned in tender admiration.

"I love you," he says.

Wait. What?

My heart stops.

Did he just drop the L-bomb?

I take a deep breath … and then another. I'm blinking at him, waiting for him to take it back but he doesn't. He's just staring at me. That smile fades, but he's still looking at me in a sweet way.

Am I supposed to say it back?

Yes, that's the polite thing to do.

No one wants to be left hanging when they declare their love for someone. I'm supposed to be feeling something too. Either butterflies in my stomach or tears streaming down my face. I could just get naked. That seems like an appropriate response. I'll do that, and then we can bypass this little lip slip until it's appropriate to discuss.

My phone rings, and answering it is an even better idea. Now. Right now.

I roll out of his arms so fast I'm surprised I didn't fall off the bed. "Hello?" I say, sounding out of breath.

"We're downstairs!" Charisse yells into the receiver.

I push the button to let them in and then glance at Jake, not sure what just happened and glad that I was saved by the bell—literally.

"Charisse and Melody are here." I put my phone back down on the nightstand. He lifts his arm as I move to the edge and stand up, fixing my clothes and smoothing down my hair. "It's our girls' night in. I forgot about it. Shoot. I don't even have anything in my cabinets."

He stands up and runs his hands up and down my arms. "Don't stress. I'm the master party guy. I have food and plenty of cider for us to serve."

"You're staying?" I pinch my brows, not sure what to think.

He gives me the sweetest grin. "Yeah. I want to meet your friends."

"But it's girls' night in." I bite my lower lip.

"Aren't they a couple?

"Yes."

"Aren't *we* a couple?"

"Yes. But you're a boy."

"A man," he corrects me in a very serious tone, and it makes me laugh.

I close my eyes, overwhelmed for all the wrong reasons. "No, you're right. I want you to officially meet my friends." There's a knock at the door. "That's them. Looks like we're making it couples' night in."

He takes my hand in his and tilts his head toward the entry way. "Let's go greet your friends."

I open the door, and I put on a fake smile, greeting my friends. "Hey, come in."

"Jake!" they both announce in unison when they see him by my side.

Clearly, they're surprised he's here.

"Jake, you met Charisse, but this is her wife, Melody." I point to Melody.

"It's nice to meet you." They shake hands before Jake asks, "Where's this beautiful daughter I've heard so much about?"

They both smile and each hold up a bottle of wine.

"She's with Grandma! We're here to relax and have the night off," Charisse says, shaking her jacket off.

"I hope you don't mind if I crash your girls' night." Jake takes it from her.

Mel looks at him with a pleasantly surprised grin.

"Mind?" she says. "Honey, I've been dying to meet you. Charisse got a good look a few weeks ago. All I've had to go by is the picture on the Moreau Flowers website."

"Melody!" I chide as Jake laughs deeply.

"You stalked me?" he asks.

"Hell yes. I had to show her the man who was taking up Lacey's time and attention. Very nice headshot, by the way. I didn't know you were a floral designer. And your family is adorable. The picture of you and your parents on the About page is so swoony," Charisse defends.

"Agreed." Melody walks toward the buffet in my dining area with her bottle of wine and takes out an opener. "I've ordered from you before, but I've never been inside. We'll have to discuss ideas for my corporate holiday party in a few months. I'd much rather give the business to someone I know. And I expect the friends-and-family discount."

"Of course," he says easily as he joins Melody.

Jake takes the bottle from her hands and starts to open it while she grabs four glasses. They're talking about flowers and wine as I pull Charisse into the kitchen. I peek past her shoulder to make sure Jake isn't facing us.

"You look like a maniac. What are you doing?" she asks as I pull her down toward my lower cabinets.

We're now squatting on the floor as I do one more look to make sure he's not peering this way.

My eyes open wide when I whisper out, "He told me he loves me."

A huge grin wraps around her face as she covers her mouth, so she doesn't squeal. After her initial glee wears off, she says, "That's amazing. I'm so happy for you."

I slap her hand. "Are you kidding me? This is crazy. We just started dating."

"What's crazy is you. Right now. You've always been quirky, but this is a little too dramatic, even for a woman who writes dramatic romance."

She stands up and looks down at me like I'm a child. I stand and brush my hands on the back of my jeans.

"There are many reasons why this is wrong. Maybe he's an obsessive lover who uses it too freely. The words lose their meaning."

"Does he strike you as the serial lover boy?"

I huff, "He dates a lot but no. It just seems too soon. Like we're still in the *getting to know you* stage. The game is over."

"Game?"

"Does he, does he not—"

"You're being ridiculous. And scared. You've known each other for a while now. Maybe not personally, but this means, he's been pining after you. He's just happy to finally get what he wants."

I give her a deadpan expression. "You can't be serious. I just don't think it's—"

"What? Possible to know when you've found the one?" she interrupts me. "Did he expect you to say it back?"

Biting my lip, I answer, "No."

She places her hand on my arm. "Don't push him away. He seems like a really good guy. It's possible you found a genuine man. They do exist. I promise. My dad was one of them." Our eyes meet, and she places her other hand on my other arm. "Stop freaking out and enjoy the moment, will ya?"

I nod and give her a weak smile, my skin prickling. We grab our glasses, and there's a pretty good chance I'll drink way too much wine tonight.

Charisse and I join Melody and Jake, who are now in my living room. Someone put music on, and they're in a pretty active conversation for two people who just met each other.

"You didn't tell us Jake's family has a cottage on the lake," Melody accuses as I come into view.

All of the wonderful memories instantly flood through me, and I can't help but smile. I slide next to Jake on the couch. "Yeah, it's beautiful. We had a lot of fun."

Charisse winks at Melody, making me hold up my finger to point at them.

"No way. This night went from girls' night to double-date night, which means there's no way we're discussing our sex life," I say.

They instantly clink their glasses together as Melody sings, "That means our girl is getting laid!"

"I told you that TikTok video was a genius idea," Charisse says.

Jake's eyes meet mine, and I can see confusion written all over his face. "That wasn't your idea?"

Melody responds, "I'll admit, I was against the idea, but it looks like my wife knows a thing or two about playing matchmaker."

Jake drops his shoulders, but that smile is still on his face. I wonder if he thought that was me breaking the ice between us. If Charisse is right and he's liked me for a while, no wonder he kissed me back. She must feel proud of herself that we're all sitting here right now. It might not have happened if it wasn't for that kissing video.

My eyes meet Charisse's, and her smile fades slightly as she looks to Jake, who has his head down as he checks his phone—the first time he's ever done so in my presence like this.

"Oh!" Charisse jumps up. "That reminds me. I saw another video that I thought you two should do together."

Jake sets his phone down, and his brows rise in intrigue. I know he loved seeing the comments and being a part of that video, so I'm sure he'd be up for the idea of doing another one.

"I tried to get this girl to do a dancing one, but she never wanted to learn the steps on her own."

"And you wouldn't do them with me!" I speak up, defending myself.

Charisse gives me a shit-eating grin. "You're right. I won't do them with you, but I bet Jake here would."

We all look to Jake, who's always the one to play along.

"I'm in. What does it entail?"

"Well, I thought this one would be fun because you don't have to really memorize certain moves—"

"Thank God!" I interrupt.

"What? You can't dance?" Jake scoots closer to me, nudging me with his leg.

"Hey, I can dance. I just hate having to do it exactly

the way they want you to. I don't have time to learn an entire dance for a two-minute video."

"Exactly why this one is great. You only have to remember the moves Jake does right before you. It's called the Last Move, First Move Challenge. So, you'll do a dance move, and then he'll repeat it and add another one of his own. Then, the camera is back on you, and you have to do his dance move and then add another one of your own, and so on and so on for as long as you want the video to go."

Jake stands, holding his hand out to me. "Sounds like fun. You game?"

I grin and place my hand in his. He pulls me close to him, and my body covers in tingles from having him pressed against me. I inhale a quick breath, and he gives me a kiss and then slaps me on the ass.

"Let's do this. Show me your moves."

"Does it have to be to a certain song?" I ask.

"Nope, you get to choose. What are we thinking?" she says, holding up her phone like she's ready to search for it.

" 'Let's Get it On'?" Jake says as he seductively pulls me in.

I laugh and push him away. "Way too slow. We need one that has a beat to dance to. Do 'Savage' by Megan Thee Stallion with Beyoncé."

"Oh yeah, we can get *nasty* in here," Jake says, using one of the lyric's words, raising his eyebrows.

I hear Melody and Charisse laugh as Charisse pulls up the song.

"So, do you want to go first, or should I?" I ask.

"This is all you, girl. Show me what you got, and I'll follow along."

We set up to where we're both in the frame right next to each other as I rub my lips together and go over some dance moves in my head.

"You guys ready?" Charisse asks.

I nod as Jake claps his hands together.

"Hell yes!"

I turn to him with a huge smile on my face from just seeing his excitement. He truly wants to do this, and I love how outgoing he is in every situation.

The song starts with Megan more speaking than singing before the beat drops, so I allow for them to be said, grinning over to Jake while the camera's rolling so whoever sees the video gets that he's my man and we're about to do this.

When the song says, "*I'm a savage*," I bust out, moving my body to the side like a snake, ending with a slight kick to my leg, like I'm tossing it to Jake.

Jake picks it right up and repeats the move, sending another one back to me. I easily repeat his move and bring my dance up a notch. His face cracks me up as he opens his mouth, trying to act all sexy as he slides his body through the motions. When he tosses it back to me, it's with a kiss blown. I do his exact movement, including the blown kiss, and when I finish my move, it just so happens to be when the song talks about gagging, so I fake like I'm choking because I took him in too deep. It catches him so off guard that he cracks up.

Instead of repeating my dance moves, he swoops me up in his arms, kissing me like no one's around or we aren't filming this to share with the world.

When he pulls back, I hear Charisse and Melody high-five as Charisse says, "Yes! Absolutely post that shit!"

CHAPTER TWENTY

We stayed up way too late last night, finishing off both bottles of wine as well as a few bottles of the hard cider Jake had bought the other day. My cheeks started hurting more than ever from the laughter we all shared. It really was the best night I'd had in a while.

When my phone rings this morning though, I have to remember just how much fun it was because my head is pounding into my skull, screaming at me at just how un-fun a hangover is.

"Hello?" I ask, trying not to strain my voice.

"Girl, you'd better get your butt out of bed because I—your wonderful, amazing agent—just so happen to be having brunch right now with Claudia Shea from Winston Arms. And, yes, I slyly slipped her your manuscript. She started reading it at the table just to appease me, but twenty minutes later, she's still reading! I snuck away to the restroom to call you. If you can get your ass here quickly, we can make this deal happen for sure."

I quickly sit up in bed as everything she said sinks in. "Shut up!" I exclaim and then grab my head, regretting my movement instantly.

Jake sits up, curious as to who I'm talking to. I cover the receiver, turn to Jake, and whisper, "It's Wendy, my agent. She loved the pages I sent her!"

"Of course she did," he says, grinning from ear to ear at my happiness.

"And now, she's sitting with a big publisher at a café, and she wants me to meet her."

"Um, who's that, and how come I didn't know you were seeing anyone?" Wendy asks.

I smile big. "That's Jake."

"Well, if he was any kind of muse for this book, I need to meet this new man of yours," she says.

My eyes roam over to Jake. His expression proves he's just as excited as I am, and he's dying for me to fill him in on what she's saying to me.

I give Jake a quick kiss and curl up in his arms. "You will," I say to Wendy.

"Okay, well, tell your new boy toy sorry, but he has to wait because you need to come down to greet your new future! Can we say *three-book deal*?" Wendy sings into the phone.

"Really?" I cover my mouth with my hand.

"Girl, you knocked this last one out of the park. It's so real, fresh. I loved every minute, and I shared it all with her. Now, get up, down some coffee to wipe away whatever hangover you're dealing with, and get down to Lula Café to join us."

"Wait. I can't just happen to be walking by and see you. That's so cliché."

"Pfft. Yes, you totally can. This is how deals are made, my friend. Get here and in front of this woman's face. She's gonna love you and the ideas for the next series you have planned."

"But I don't have a next series planned."

"You will by the time you get here. Now, let's get you a deal."

She hangs up, and I have to sit here for a second to absorb what she just said.

"Ahh!" I scream, not caring one bit how bad it hurts. Okay, well, I do care because it's throbbing.

Jake chuckles under his breath as I grab my head. "You go shower while I get some Advil and water for you."

I fall onto the bed and sigh. "I can't believe she liked it so much!"

"Of course she did. I never doubted she would." He flips me around in his arms, so I'm on top of him. I feel his length beneath me, and I instinctively grind into him. "We need to celebrate."

I sigh as I push myself up. "Hold that thought. Celebratory sex will have to wait. Help yourself to any breakfast and grab my laptop to watch a movie or something. I'll be back shortly."

"Are you saying you want me naked, in your bed, waiting for you to come home?"

"Yes, that's exactly what I'm saying."

He grips my hips and holds me still. "Sex is definitely in the cards, but I was talking about a date. I want to take my girl out tonight. Maybe some drinks and dancing. A night where we get dressed up and hit the town."

His smirk makes me want to stay home and forget meeting Wendy altogether.

I lean up to kiss his lips. "A date, huh?"

"A real one. Not the kind where one of us is trying to prove something to the other."

With a grin on my face, I nod in acceptance. "Jake Moreau, I will absolutely go on a real date with you." With a quick kiss, I get up and rush into the bathroom for a shower.

I get ready with rapid speed. Jake is still in the bed, wrapped up in my sheets, watching me with a grin on his face. On the nightstand is the Advil and water he promised would be there when I got out of the shower.

I pop the pills and drink the entire full glass. Then, I lean down to kiss him good-bye.

"Love you," he says, and this time, I can't ignore it.

I don't know how to respond to that, but he's staring at me with his eyes narrowing slightly as he looks at my puckered face.

He tilts his head with a soothing glance. "It's okay, Lace. You don't have to say it back."

"It's just … it's sudden. We've only been dating for a few days. Seriously, like, one week really, and it feels so—"

"Sudden. Yes, I know."

"Very. And you see … well, I just don't think you love me as much as you lust for me."

"Excuse me?" He sits up in bed fully.

"Great sex is often confused with love."

His mouth pinches, and I know I hit a nerve with that one.

"I know what love is. The question is, do you?"

"I don't do love, Jake." My tone is entirely rude, but not on purpose. I care about this man deeply. "Shit. Sorry. This is not how I wanted to have this conversation and certainly not now when I'm rushing off to a really important meeting. Can we talk about this when I get back? Stay here. Or if you go home, I'll knock, but please, let's have this conversation later today."

"Yeah." He takes a deep breath. "Go. Good luck."

I lean in to kiss him, and thankfully, he kisses me back, though it's short and rushed.

"I won't be long."

I race out the door and down to my car. Once I know my phone is connected through the Bluetooth, I dial Charisse.

"I'm a horrible mom this morning, thanks to you," she says as her hello.

"My agent loved the book, and she's having brunch with someone from Winston Arms, so I'm rushing to meet them, but before I left, Jake said *it* again."

"Whoa, wait. That's a lot to take in after everything we drank last night. So, first, OMG! Congratulations. That's super exciting. I'm talking about Winston Arms *and* Jake being candid with his feelings."

"Yes, but …"

"But what, Lacey? Stop pretending you don't love him too. I was there last night. I saw the way you two looked at each other. It's obvious that he loves you. Even if you hadn't told me he said so, I would have thought it. Stop fighting this. You're getting your dream career the same time you found your dream man. You need to sit back and enjoy life, not worry about what might or might not happen."

I sit silently as I drive down the road. My mind is a mess with everything that's going on. I'm so freaking happy yet so absolutely terrified that something has to go wrong because it's all too good.

"Get out of your head," Charisse says when I don't say anything. "Let every single thing happen with Jake. And treasure it!"

I let out a deep exhale.

"Now, tell me about this publishing house," she says like the Jake topic is solved and over with and it's time to move on to the next.

The meeting went amazing even though I felt really awkward, just appearing to be in the same area. My acting skills were severely lacking. Thankfully, I was ushered into a seat, and the three of us discussed romance tropes and writing styles like we'd been in the same book club for years. A few Bloody Marys later—which were tremendous for getting rid of my hangover—we talked ideas for a book series I could write.

Between the three of us, we came up with a story line that was unique and filled a niche the publisher was looking for. I didn't have a deal yet, so when Wendy started kicking my ankle under the table, I knew she wanted me to skedaddle, so she could start the negotiations groundwork.

On the way back to the apartment, I envision all the exciting things I'm going to do to Jake and what he's going to do to me. For a lady who hasn't had sex in years, I am certainly looking forward to trying some risqué maneuvers. The pretzel, the X-position, and the human wheelbarrow are at the top of my list. I've written about these sexy moves but never tried them. Now, I have a smokin'-hot man to experiment with.

When I arrive home, I notice my apartment is quiet. *So much for him waiting in bed.* I suppose it would be rude for me to expect him to stay there for three hours.

I rush over to his place, knocking on the door. There are no footsteps or movements on the other side. I knock again, and when it still goes unanswered, I head to the front of our apartment complex, where I can see out of the window to where he normally parks his car. He's not here.

Bummed, I reach for my phone and click on his name. The phone rings until I get his voice mail. I leave him a playful message as I head to my couch, wondering if he left me a note or anything.

Five hours later, I still have no idea where he is. I could call the flower shop, but I don't want to come off like a needy girlfriend. So, I'll just wait.

And still …

Something doesn't feel right. When I saw him this morning, he was sexy and sweet.

And he said he loved me.

I told him it was too soon, that it was only lust, and he seemed fine. He *was* fine, wasn't he? Yes, he didn't take too kindly to me assuming he didn't know what love was. But who would? Some say it's a feeling you get, but feelings are fleeting. People outgrow the way they think every day. Others believe love is physical. Both carnal and nurturing. In both cases, I can love a man as much as I love ice cream or a puppy. It's all so easy to dismiss when the puppy is gone, the ice cream is eaten, and the man walks away.

Running my hands through my hair, I walk to my kitchen and grab a bottle of wine. I have no idea where he went, and I need to prepare myself for the truth that he might be second-guessing this whole thing.

CHAPTER TWENTY-ONE

As I drink my coffee to try to make up for the sleep I didn't get due to worrying about Jake all night, there's a knock at my door.

I open it to see Jake looking no better than me on the other end. He's still handsome, hair coiffed and his clothes looking straight out of a catalog, but those chocolate-brown eyes are glazed and tired.

Either he stayed up until the sun went down or he never came home. Yes, I checked multiple times last night—even as late as three o'clock in the morning—to see if his car was here, and it never was.

"Where have you been? I was worried," I say, reaching my arms up to give him a hug.

As I hold him, his body feels looser than it usually does when I'm near him. It's like he's putting in very little effort.

As I step back from his arms, I see he's carrying a large stack of printed papers.

"Can we talk?" he asks.

I invite him in without saying anything. He heads toward the kitchen, where he puts the stack of papers down and leans his hip against my counter. He crosses his arms as he inhales, still planning out his words. I give him the time to say what he needs to say as we stand in silence together.

"What is that?" I point to the papers.

"It's *The Artist*."

My eyes bug out of my head, as I didn't expect him to have a copy of my book. "Where did you get that?"

"Charisse."

I'm at a total loss for words. I knew he was going to read it eventually, but I didn't tell him he was my muse. That said, I assumed when I did tell him, he'd get a huge kick out of it. I wasn't prepared for him to show up here, looking so downhearted. He's upset, but I still can't figure out why.

He meets my eyes. Keeping his body language closed, he asks, "How come you freaked out when I told you how I felt about you?"

I tilt my head in confusion. Here I thought, this had to do with the book, but this is not what I figured he would ask first.

I close my eyes and make my way to the cupboard, reaching for a mug. "Can I get you a cup of coffee?"

He places his hand on mine, stopping my movements. "I don't need coffee. I want an answer." He picks up the book. "Is this how you feel? Obviously, I'm your hero, and this book is our entire relationship with everything we've done together, so I ask, is this how you feel about me?"

I bite on my thumb, and he pulls it out of my mouth, staring straight into my eyes, waiting for my answer.

"I don't know yet," I say under my breath as I turn away.

He moves around the counter to where I am and stands in front of me, making sure he's my sole focus. "So, you're saying I'm good enough to use to write a story, but I'm not good enough to be in love with?"

My shoulders fall as I tilt my head up to him. "That's not what happened, and you know it."

He raises his eyebrows, and he steps back to give me my space. "Explain it to me because it sounds like you took our entire relationship from the day we met and turned it into a love story."

"I thought you'd be happy about that." I place my hand on his chest, but it's obvious my touch is not welcome, so I pull it back.

"You thought I'd be happy about the fact that you think our life was good enough for fiction, yet you're not sure if you believe in what you write? Do you even like me, or was this just to get story ideas since you were suffering from writer's block?"

"You know it wasn't like that. I'm crazy about you." I step toward him, but he puts his hands up, silently asking me to stay where I am.

"No, I don't. I told you I was in love with you, and you freaked out."

"You can't love me. No one falls that fast. Besides, that's not love; it's lust and some fun jokes and great moments, but that doesn't mean it's going to last."

"Bullshit."

He steps closer, and I take in a sharp inhale.

"Excuse me?"

"You fell in love with me too." He's even closer now, and I can barely breathe, having him so near.

"You sound so sure," I say under my breath as I reach for my cup to have some kind of security even if it's false.

"You did, Lacey." He places his fingers under my chin to turn my face back toward him. "You fell in love with me, and it's right here in all two hundred and eight fucking pages. You think love doesn't last? Well, even you gave us a damn epilogue, saying it did."

"It's fiction," I yell as tears prick my eyes, mad that they're appearing.

"It's reality, and you're scared. Admit it. You're afraid of what this is. It's love. It's you and me, and it's happening. Yes, couples fight. Yes, they probably even hate each other's guts some days. But that's the real world. Loving someone so damn much that you'll weather through the storm is what I want. I'm willing to try that with you, but you're not."

"No, that's not true." I shake my head as I let everything he just said sink in. "You're too much of a dreamer, Jake. You can't even see that what we have is moving so fast. Too fast. I mean, who even says *I love you* this soon?"

"You do. It's right here in your book." He slaps his hand on the pages.

"Stop throwing my book in my face."

"You don't think you're a walking hypocrite? You're still on birth control, Lace. Why? And don't give me some bullshit about how it regulates your period. You're hiding behind the fact that you still care about meeting someone. Being intimate with someone."

"Sex is not love."

"It was for me. With you, it was love. I wasn't even expecting for you to say it back. I knew you wouldn't be able to. Not yet, anyway. Yet, you couldn't even handle me expressing it. You can't handle a man feeling love toward you."

"I can only give you so much of me," I say as tears fill my eyes. "Why can't you be okay with what I'm willing to give?"

"You have no idea how cruel you are."

I shake my head again as tears fall down my face. "Don't say that—"

"You used me."

"How can you say that? You wanted me to write about you. *Let me be your muse. I'm the perfect book boyfriend. A total catch.* You are so two-faced, you know that? You want me to write about you, and when I do, you flip. You wanted this. Admit it."

"Not like this."

"Then, like what then?"

"You'll never get it. I'm not going to stand here and fight for you to love me." He walks around me and heads toward the front of my apartment.

"That's right. Run. Your mother's right. You are a typical Libra who can't handle not being the center of attention. If you're not the center of my damn universe, then you don't want in at all. I'm willing to give you what I can. It's you who wants more. Well, we're not Cassiopeia and Cepheus. I'm not going to fling myself into the heavens for some egomaniac."

NAUGHTY NEIGHBOR

He stops to glare at me, and I know I've gone too far.

When he turns to leave again without saying another word, I try to stop him. "Wait, Jake. Don't go."

"Good-bye, Lace."

"Fuck. No. Wait. I'm sorry. I didn't mean it."

He stops and turns again. "You know what your problem is? You're stuck in your own head. And I'm not talking about your stories. Your past and why you're living this lie are totally bullshit. I'm not Michael. I'm not your father or that stupid fuck you lost your virginity to in high school. I'm Jake Moreau, and up until five minutes ago, I was convinced I was in love with you. Call me insecure, but, yeah, when I'm with a woman, I want to be her whole damn world, and I refuse to be punished for wanting so. Damn, you have so much to love, Lacey; it's a shame you can't even see it."

"Jake—"

He keeps walking and then says over his shoulder, "Don't come knocking on my door. I won't be there."

"Can't you just—"

He slams the door in my face, stopping me suddenly. I place my palms on it and let the tears fall freely.

You don't realize the power someone has over you until they leave you. I protected myself from getting hurt again, only to find my heart more broken than it's ever been.

This is why I don't do relationships. Every great romance has a breakup scene. In fiction, you can write about the couple getting back together. In the real world, they slam doors and hate each other.

I don't need him, I tell myself. *Then, why do I feel so fucking miserable?*

232

I walk back into my kitchen, this time not wanting a cup of coffee. I need the hard stuff. As I'm grabbing a glass, I see the damn manuscript on the counter. Instead of the title page being on top, there's a printout of an email. It's from Charisse and addressed to Jake at the flower shop.

Lifting it up, I read the subject line.

For Jake Moreau only.

In the body is a simple message:

Don't let her convince you she doesn't believe in love. She does. And you're the man who changed her.

For the first time in years, I cry.

A tear falls because of my meddling best friend who had to go and stick her nose in my business.

More come as I remember how used I felt when Michael walked out the door.

I sob when I think about my father and how he barely put forth the effort to be my dad.

That feeling I had the other day in the car, the one where I felt the ground leaving me, is back. Except, this time, I can't hold on to my chest and steady it. My entire insides feel like they're dropping down to my feet.

I'm falling apart. Body and soul, I come undone as I realize the only man I was willing to put my heart on the line for walked away from me, like everyone else.

CHAPTER TWENTY-TWO

JAKE

I'm the kind of guy who is looking for his dream girl. For me, she's a classically put together, ultra-feminine woman who is polite, alluring, and socially confident.

That's why when Lacey Camille "Rivers" Wampo knocked on my door a few years ago, I wasn't worried about her stealing my heart. Her hair was a mess, she had a stain on the front of her sweatshirt, and one look at me in that seafoam-green towel left her speechless—and not in the captivating way. She was a fumbling mess, but it made me smile.

While she certainly left an impression, I wasn't going to hit on my elusive neighbor, especially when she seemed to go out of her way to avoid me at all costs. Sure, she said the casual hello—when it was rude not to. And if my mail was left in her slot, she'd kindly send it my way.

NAUGHTY NEIGHBOR

Did I think she was cute? Hell yes. She had long brown hair, big green eyes, and a gorgeous smile, but I never planned to touch her.

Then, she knocked on my door the night of my party.

Man, her fist could have taken the thing down. I was going to say something witty when I opened the door and saw her hand still in the air, ready to rattle the steel, but the one-liner I had prepared vanished.

There was something about her then.

When she showed up at my door, looking a mess—yet sexy as hell—I knew I was in trouble. Her skin was flush, her eyes were large and bright, and those lips were puckered, drawing my attention to how full they were.

Now, I love to dress nice, and I appreciate a woman who does, too, yet there was no denying the way her breasts looked in that tank top and how the yoga pants hugged her hips. Yes, I always thought she was cute, but in that moment, something clicked.

It might have been the determined attitude she had. A woman on a mission was sexy as fuck. Then, I found out she was a romance novelist, and my intrigue level surged. She was the creative type, and I wanted to learn more.

I kept our greetings friendly, but every time I saw her in the hall, I'd spend the rest of the night thinking about her, wondering what she did all day in that apartment of hers. I wanted so badly to get to know her better, and slowly but surely, that wall I kept up, keeping her as my friendly—yet cute—neighbor, broke away piece by piece.

When I found myself in Lacey's apartment, getting

limejuice for the yoga instructor I had planned to take to bed that night, all I wanted to do was sit and talk to *her*, get to know *her*. I had a sure thing waiting for me, and I couldn't have cared less. When I got back to my place, I cut the date short and ended up driving her home after one drink. I knew my head was focused on Lacey, and I wasn't going to string anyone else along.

Then, she kissed me.

Holy fucking shit, did she kiss me.

Her lips were like velvety cushions, and her tongue tasted of wine. My hands caressed those curves I knew she liked to hide, and, damn, I wanted to touch them all.

Maybe it was because Lacey was a hard girl to read, but I fell for her cat-and-mouse tease. She wouldn't just go out with me. Everything became a game—a series of us telling each other what to do and seeing if the other would go along with it. They might have been more friends hanging out than dates, but with each, I fell harder every time.

Lacey thinks we've only been dating a week, yet she had me at a ferocious knock on the door.

I thought she was as into me as I was into her.

Finding out the TikTok kiss wasn't even her idea, I'm not gonna lie, it stung. Here I thought, she was finally giving in to the same attraction I'd felt all this time, only to learn I was merely the closest available guy.

I'm such an idiot.

I pull up to the cottage, needing to get away. Both of my sisters' cars are here, and I consider driving off, but I have nowhere else to go. Plus, I actually like my family. Having them around isn't a burden at all.

"What are you doing here?" Milène asks when I walk inside.

"Felt like getting away for a few. Why are you still here?"

"Wayne's parents decided to keep the kids a few extra days. They'll be coming up tomorrow." She takes my duffel bag and puts it on the chair in the foyer. "You hungry? We had meatloaf for dinner, and there's plenty of leftovers."

"No, thanks. I'm good." I keep my tone even. I don't want to ruin anyone's day with my melodrama. "Who else is here?"

"Just me, Wayne, and Penelope. She's heading out tomorrow. We're all like a bunch of ships passing in the night. It's amazing we can keep track of who's coming and going." She laughs as I follow her into the kitchen. "I thought you had to be at the shop."

"I was. I worked today and then drove here."

She washes her hands in the sink. "Everything okay at your apartment?"

Grabbing a beer from the refrigerator, I pop the top and wonder if I should share my bullshit with her. "I'm just looking for some space."

"Damn it," she says with a huff.

"What?"

"You broke up," she states, looking genuinely disappointed. "I really liked this one. She's not like some of the princesses you've brought around. Lacey was so down-to-earth."

So down-to-earth, yet she refuses to let her heart out of her concrete chest.

"Well, we had a disagreement, and for the record,

her best friend is on my side, so I know I did nothing wrong."

"What does she think you did?"

"Told her I loved her." I take a swig and watch my sister's mouth form an O in understanding.

I'm drinking, and Milène is still making that face as Wayne comes in.

"What's up, brother?" he says. We slap hands, and then Wayne grabs a beer from the fridge. "What brings you here tonight?"

"He and Lacey broke up."

Wayne looks at his wife, confused. "They were just here, banging in the hot tub."

"Wayne!" she chastises, and I have to laugh.

"Didn't think anyone heard that," I say with a grin, recalling that night. It's amazing how my relationship with Lacey went from that to this.

Wayne laughs. "Just us. Our window is right above the hot tub. This one"—he points to his wife—"wanted the window open to get the lake breeze. She got that and a few moans."

While my relationship with my sister is really good, this is a little too intimate, even for me. "Lucky for you, you won't be hearing any more of that. She and I are through."

Wayne raises a shoulder. "No big deal. You probably have another woman lined up already."

"He told her he loved her," Milène explains, but Wayne doesn't seem affected.

"Shit happens. The guy knows half of Chicago. I'm sure he can get laid pretty easily and forget her." Wayne's words do not appear to be going over well with Milène.

I interject before she yells at him, "The guy's right. In fact, I should make it a point and bring as many women as possible home with me, so I can walk past her door and let her see just how desirable I am to other women."

Wayne lifts his beer to cheers me. "That's a horrible idea, but I will support it." We tap the necks of our bottles and then take a drink. With his mouth hidden behind the bottle, he mumbles toward me, "I'm only saying it's horrible because my wife is standing right there."

Milène crumples a napkin and throws it at his head. "You're a fool."

The two bicker, which turns into some funny jabs at each other. That's the way they are. They fight like an old married couple yet still laugh like they did when they first started dating.

"Come on, Jake. We're going out." Wayne puts his bottle on the counter and starts walking out of the kitchen. He talks over his shoulder, "Honey, don't wait up. I'm doing my brother-in-law duty and getting this guy out of his slump."

"I'm not in a slump, but I'll come out." I toss my empty bottle in the recycling bin and follow him out the front door.

"Don't drink and drive," Milène calls out to us. "Take an Uber home if you must. We'll get the car in the morning."

He turns back and gives his wife a kiss good-bye, thanking her for being the best, which is all just to butter her up because she really is a great wife to him. The guy lives a pretty carefree life.

We get to the bar, and it's slightly packed. The music is blaring, and the drinks are flowing. Wayne and I take a seat at the bar and order draft beers.

We shoot the shit for the most part. Last week's football game. Yesterday's baseball game. He tells me he saw *Hamilton* on the television, and we talk about history for a while.

"So, you're really hung up on this girl?" he asks on our second round.

I bring the bottle to my lips, saying, "Yep," before I take a drink.

"Listen, I get it. I've been a sucker for Milène since I first met her. You don't have to explain instant love to me. I might act like a buffoon, but that woman has me wrapped around her finger. Did you notice she finally got me to cut my hair?"

I nod as I look at his new style. The guy had taken a break from cutting it and was starting to achieve a mullet.

He runs his hand through the short locks. "The things you do for women."

A hard, quick laugh escapes my lips. "I believe it. I would have shaved my head if Lacey had asked, and trust me when I say, I do not have any desire to chop this off." I run my hands through my thick hair. I have good hair and would like to keep it.

"So, what happened?"

I lean back in the chair and shrug. "She doesn't do relationships, yet we found ourselves deep into one real quick."

"Then, what?"

"I told her how I felt, and she freaked out."

He chuckles under his breath. "You're telling me that after all the women you've dated, you finally found someone worth sticking around for, and she's the one who broke it off?"

"Actually, I think she would have been fine, living in her bubble."

Wayne knocks his knuckles on the wood as he looks down at the bar. "Well, if you want a distraction, there's a pretty little redhead with her eyes on you."

I glance down the bar and see just that. A very attractive woman with curly red hair is smiling at me. "You really think a one-night stand will do the trick?"

"Hell if I know. I've never had one, but if you could fall for Lacey so fast, maybe you'll surprise yourself by meeting your next dream girl tonight."

I have doubts I'll feel better after doing this, but I get off the stool, walk over to the redhead, and introduce myself.

"Catrina," she says and extends a hand. "You from around here?"

"Chicago. You?"

"Same. I'm an interior designer."

"Florist." I hold up my beer and nod.

And this is how it goes. Catrina is here with friends, who are at a table, talking. She was just at the bar, getting a drink, when she saw me. She's single and in her late twenties, and she lives with her cat. She's wearing a pretty green dress, and she's very talkative. Interesting even.

She's a classically put together, ultra-feminine woman who is polite, alluring, and socially confident.

But she's no Lacey.

While Catrina is talking, I'm picturing Lacey in that golden dress, the one she wore on the date with the guy who wasn't me. The thought of her going out with another man and wearing that damn dress eats away at me. She looked so gorgeous that night. Hell, I found her stunning in just a pair of sweats. You can't hide beauty like hers. Not under all the wine stains in the world.

As Catrina practically purrs as she speaks, I can still hear Lacey's voice. She has this shy quality to it when she's uncomfortable or nervous. That's when I knew she liked me, and later, I found it was the same when she was turned on. Her voice was breathy, and it made me wild.

As I got to know Lacey more, she was more than polite, alluring, and confident. She was funny and sincere. Her joy was found in things she loved and in what I wanted to do. I could experience life with Lacey. Conversations never had a lull, and when we were in silence, we were content.

And the sex … fuck, the sex was amazing. Maybe I'm the fool. I should have just lived in her loveless bubble and had all the sex I wanted. That way, I could get her mind and her body.

But I'd never have her heart.

Catrina is talking about something, and I feel like shit because I spaced out. I have no idea what she was saying.

"I'm sorry. Can you repeat that?" I ask her.

"My friends want to stay, but I want to get out of here. I have to be up early."

I know it's bullshit. She wants me to offer to bring her home, and it will be followed by an invitation up to her place. I know this is a line because I've heard it before. And I've gone along with it.

Tonight, I don't have it in me.

"I can give you the number to a local taxi company," I offer, and she looks displeased.

"You wouldn't happen to be heading out anytime soon, would you?" she asks, batting her lashes.

I turn around and look at Wayne, who's watching us with interest. He'll probably tell me I'm crazy for turning her down. The guy has never had the carefree bachelor life and lives vicariously through me.

"No. I'll be hanging with my brother-in-law for a while. I should get back to him. It was nice meeting you." I turn around and go back to Wayne, who's staring at me with raised brows and his arms out. I shake my head. "She's getting over a bad breakup and not looking for anything right now. If you're good to go, I am too. I'm really tired."

Like a good friend, he just nods, tosses some peanuts from the bowl on the bar into his mouth, and slaps a twenty on the bar for the bartender as a tip. "Let's get out of here then."

When we get home, I thank him for his company, and he heads up to his room. I might have said I was tired before, but the truth is, I'm wired, so I get another drink from the refrigerator and head out to the back deck.

The stars are bright tonight. I sit in an Adirondack chair and look up at the constellations.

"Hey, bro."

I'm startled as Penelope appears, heading over to the seat next to me. She nudges my leg and then sits beside me.

I glance in her direction. "I take it, Milène told you, so I don't have to fill you in?"

She nods. "She did. You okay?"

I shrug and look back up at the stars, of course seeing Cassiopeia staring back at me. "I'm okay with her not saying she loves me back. I get it. But I need to know that she might love me one day. She couldn't even give me that."

"What did she say?"

"She called me an egomaniac. Said I needed to be the center of attention. You know what? She's right. What's so bad about wanting to be the sole focus of the woman you're with? She knew this about me really early on, and then she threw it in my face like it was a bad thing."

"Did you know that she didn't believe in love?"

My sister's comment earns her an intense side-eye from me.

"Not exactly. She says she doesn't believe in love, yet her entire living is based around that mere fact. I called her a hypocrite. I'm pissed that she believes it enough to write about it, yet she's afraid to actually live it."

"Whoa … so shit got deep then." She sits back fully in the chair and looks up at the stars the same way I am.

She doesn't say a word as I continue to drink my beer and count my favorite constellations.

Eventually, she lets out a sigh.

"Did I tell you I've read all of her books?" she says, and I turn to her, impressed.

"That's a lot of pages for an author you just discovered."

She raises one shoulder with a slight grin, shyly covering her face. "What can I say? I went on a binge. It's not every day your brother dates a romance writer. I thought it was cool, having actually met her."

"What did you think of the books?"

"I loved them. She's really talented. I noticed her books have different themes, but they follow the same formula. The couple meets and gets together, and then some outside drama keeps them apart. They have to fight to get back together, and the end. Yes, they're all super romantic, and the way she writes love makes you believe you'll find it someday."

"I feel a *but* coming on."

"But"—she smiles—"there's always someone who doesn't believe in love fighting against the couple. Whether it's a meddling mom or boyfriends who left the heroine scarred for life or even a father who deserted her … the conflict always revolves around the heroine saying true love doesn't exist."

When our eyes meet, I know she's thinking the same thing I am. Lacey writes about herself. She's the one who's fighting against the notion. It's like her books are her own therapy. I know, deep down, she wants it because every couple gets their happy ending, yet she's not living her own. I hate that she's onto something.

"She wrote a book about me. About us. Every single fucking detail."

"*Every* detail?" she asks slowly.

"Every. Single. One. I should be flattered. Hell, I kind of am." I turn back to face the stars. "I wanted to be her muse until I read it and saw me there. Do you think all of her heroes are old boyfriends she uses to create romance?"

She shrugs. "I don't think so or else she'd have an epic dating life that I'd envy. It seems to me, she inserts herself into her worlds, and she might not even realize she's doing it half the time."

"She knew she was doing it with us. She even gave us a happily ever after."

Penelope laughs lightly. "What was it?"

"She had us breakup—like she knew that was the next stage in our relationship—then we get back together in this big, romantic scene where I grovel for her love at the museum where I took her on our first non-date."

"I like that ending. Does it work for you? Do you want to beg for her forgiveness?"

I run my hand through my hair. "I have nothing to apologize for."

"Do you still want her?"

The question is simple and so damn complicated.

"I do, but I want someone who isn't afraid of love. A woman who is willing to put me first, and I don't care how cocky that sounds."

"May I make a suggestion?" Before I even answer, she reaches for her phone, types something in, and then hits Send.

My phone dings with an incoming email. I open it up to see Penelope just sent me a book of Lacey's through Amazon, one I hadn't read yet.

"Start with this one. It's her first book. Learn more about what's inside her head. Then, maybe you'll understand why she ticks the way she does."

"So, I read and then what? I already know why she is the way she is. She's been burned in the past, which is why she can't open up in the present."

She pats my leg as she stands up. "I was really glad you brought her home. Seeing you two together gave me hope for myself. Just don't give up on her, okay? If her books are anything like her real life, she's been let down a lot when it comes to love."

I nod. Penelope's the second person to say that to me about Lacey, the first being her friend Charisse when she told me to read the book, though I'm not sure if it's already too late.

She kisses me goodnight and heads inside. I finish my drink and stare at the dark night as I hold up my phone.

"Fuck it," I say and open the Kindle app.

Looks like I have some reading to do.

CHAPTER TWENTY-THREE

LACEY

"I feel like shit," Charisse says over the phone as I tell her for the tenth time that it's not her fault.

"Stop apologizing. You're an adorable meddler. It's in your nature."

It makes me laugh a little that I'm the one who is calming her down. But that's why she's my best friend. When Charisse gets something in her head, she acts on it. This time, it was my love life and her need to fix me.

"I know how you get, and when you told me you were freaking out about the relationship, I heard it in your voice—you were going to bail," she says, stinging me a little.

"Actually, I wasn't. Doesn't matter though. Turns out, me not seeing ourselves twenty years from now was a deal-breaker."

She groans, annoyed. "But you love him."

With my hand on my chest, I steady myself and take a breath. "I care for him deeply."

I don't know why I can't just admit that I've fallen for Jake in more ways than just caring for him. The fact that I can't breathe without thinking about what he must be doing right now shows I'm more attached to him than I thought.

Do I love Jake Moreau?

Yes, I fucking love him so much, it hurts.

I just don't know how to dig my way out of this hole of self-pity.

I haven't seen him in a week, yet it feels like a year. I went so long without him in my life, and now that he's gone, I miss him like crazy. I'd try telling him that, but then what? He's too nice of a guy. He'd come over and want to talk. He'd wind up understanding my issues, as he always did, but then we'd never move forward. He's a romantic, and I am … scared.

"Do you need me to come over? Melody will understand if I tell her you're in need of an impromptu girls' night."

Curling onto the couch, I tuck my knees into my chest and sigh. "I'm fine. I plan on watching *Inception*. Tom Hardy is so hot in that film."

"You need a new muse. That guy is old news."

I give her the finger through the receiver even though she can't see it. She seems happy that I'm in a good mood, and then we hang up.

I feel okay, too, even though the thought of a muse tugs at my gut.

My muse.

Our story was pretty epic. I didn't mean to write it

word for word, but as our friendship progressed and the relationship ensued, it felt natural. I was only going to use it as a launch point for scenes, but the feelings were jumping off the page.

It was raw.

It was real.

It was ours.

And now, it's over. Cue dramatic music and romance author sitting on her sofa with a bowl full of chocolate chip cookie dough ice cream and a sweatshirt that hasn't been washed in three days. Not my best look, I know.

Tom Hardy finally appears on the screen, only a side character in this film, when my house phone rings. It's my mother, and she's here.

Surprised by the impromptu visit, I buzz her in.

"Hey, Mom," I say when she gets off the elevator. I'm standing in my open doorway, watching her walk toward me. "Wasn't expecting you."

"I know. That's why it's called a surprise visit."

"That's also why God invented the telephone—so you could give someone a warning that you were arriving."

She walks in my apartment and raises her brow. "If I called first, would you have changed that sweatshirt?"

I look down and shrug. "Yeah, probably not. I would have set out some snacks. I don't have anything to eat. I'm down to Pringles."

"That's fine. We can order in." She takes off her coat and her shoes. There's a large tote on her shoulder that she places on my dining room table.

"Staying awhile?" I ask as I see the size of the thing.

Walking to the Keurig, she pops in a pod and grabs a mug. "Depends."

I hold my arms out and wait for her to finish her sentence. She watches the coffee drip into the mug before it makes that gurgling sound at the end. When it's ready, she grabs her coffee and walks to my living room.

I follow her in. "You going to finish that sentence? Depends on what?"

She turns her head and smiles.

I narrow my eyes.

With a pat on the sofa, she says, "I read your book. Now, sit. We need to talk."

Okay, I'm really uncomfortable with where this conversation might go. My mother is my worst critic, but she's also been a champion of my writing style. We've discussed prose and turn of phrase, but this feels like more than the intellectual chitchat.

Dragging my feet, I make my way over to the couch and take the seat she's offering on the sofa.

"Should I be concerned?" I ask her as I tuck my heels under my butt.

She sighs, something between melancholy and disappointment. "I think I've failed you."

"I don't know why you'd say such a thing. Do you think my book was *that* bad?"

"The opposite." Her mouth twists. "It was beautiful."

A surge of emotion rushes up my chest and into my eyes. I'm twirling my hand in the air in an attempt to push away the tears threatening to come up.

"Lacey, are you crying?" Even she knows this is very out of character for me.

"Yeah. It's something I've been doing a lot of lately."

Her eyes widen as she looks around, feeling equally out of place as I do. "Well then, you need a hug."

She outstretches her arm and pulls me in. It's awkward and yet so very comforting. My mom has never been a hugger per se, but she did know how to hold me when I was a child and in need of affection.

I wrap my arms around her and hug her tightly. The tears that I had are subsiding, and I'm feeling more like myself.

Sitting up straight, I take a deep breath. "Thanks for that."

She wipes a tear from my cheek. "I can tell exactly why you've been crying. This book is different. Yes, it was romance, but it didn't feel like fiction. It felt real."

I sit back and wipe my cheek. "How so?"

"Well, for starters, the heroine is afraid of love. She's been hurt by her father, her ex"—she pauses—"her mother."

Now, I know this book has more of my real life than others, but everyone is really treating this book like it's an autobiography. "You're reading too much into it."

"The story is about Jake. It doesn't take a rocket scientist to see you've fallen in love with this man. And rightfully so. He's charming, attractive, and sympathetic."

"Which means he's just setting me up before he leaves."

"Maybe." She shrugs. "Maybe not." She adjusts her hips and turns to me, so she can level her gaze with mine as she speaks sternly, "I don't trust men, and neither do you. We've been burned. That's our history. However, I don't want you to ever believe that love doesn't exist."

"I know it does. I just don't believe it will happen for me."

"That was then. Your other books all reflected that. Yes, the hero and heroine always wound up together, but it was superficial. In this book, what you have with Jake shows through. I don't know if it will last. No one does. I just want to make sure you know that I'm happy for you, and I don't want you to hide your relationship from me anymore."

I smile; it's the kind of grin that hits my eyes. Unfortunately, it falls just as fast. "We're not in a relationship. It ended."

She leans back, confused. "What about that epilogue you wrote?"

"That wasn't real. Our story ended at the cottage. In the book, the heroine realizes she's in love with him on the drive home, and, yes, that was me, but in real life, I panicked. It was all downhill from there."

She nods knowingly. "I see. Did he panic too?"

"Nope. He's pretty steadfast in his feelings."

"And you still love him?"

With a nod, I'm finally ready to say it out loud. "Very much so, yes."

"But you're scared?"

I nod again. "Very much so, yes."

"Then, there's only one more question," she says, and I look up and wait for her to ask it. "Do you love him more than you're scared?"

Closing my eyes, I smile. "I think so."

"Then, it looks like you have a new epilogue to write."

CHAPTER TWENTY-FOUR

I'm standing outside Moreau Flowers, entirely too nervous to be doing this. If Jake won't come home, then I need to go to him, and work is the most obvious place to find him.

I open the door, and the chime goes off, sounding more like a siren in my head than a sweet jangling, as it probably does to everyone else.

Jake is at the front desk, doing a floral design for a client. He's smiling that gorgeous grin I've missed and making the client laugh. His ease while working actually makes my racing heart simmer down a bit. That's just what he does. He calms you with his presence.

That is, of course, until he looks at you.

Those chocolate eyes make me melt into a puddle of goo as he stares at me.

"Hi, Lacey," he says, and I'm surprised.

The couple he's working with is standing right here. They turn around to see who he's talking to.

I give a wave. "You can get back to helping these nice people."

His eyes narrow, but his mouth tilts up as he stands straight and states nonchalantly, "It's okay. You remember my buddy Kent from the museum. And this is his fiancée, Sydney. Guys, this is Lacey."

His ease with me being here is unnerving. I thought he'd be angry or pissed. Instead, he's just … lovely.

Kent and Sydney are smiling and take a step to the side, as if to give me a path toward the counter, where Jake is working. The way Sydney grabs Kent with a big smile on her face proves to me that they know *exactly* who I am and why I'm here.

"Can I get you anything?" Jake asks, and I panic slightly.

"Um … yes. I came for daisies."

He quirks a brow. "Daisies?"

"Yes."

Without another question, he turns to the cooler behind him and takes out a bunch of the happy-looking flower. He walks them over to a side counter, where tissue paper and cellophane are ready for him to make a bouquet. My skin is prickling as I watch him make the bouquet, the entire event not going as planned. I wasn't expecting there to be people in the store, and I certainly wasn't prepared for him to squeeze me in while he was working with them.

"Here you go." He hands me the bouquet, and I get lost for a moment in how handsome he looks in his green sweater.

"Thanks."

I take out my wallet, but he holds up a hand.

"On the house."

He's acting friendly. It's not like the man who walked out of my apartment. It's like the guy who was my neighbor. This is all too easy. It's as if he's giving me an out. If I want to end things, then he'll let me, and he won't make it awkward.

I should be grateful. Yes, I'm happy with this turn of events.

Taking my flowers, I thank him again and then smile at his friends. That's what normal people do.

I turn around and head toward the door, pushing it open and hearing that bell chime.

Then, it hits me.

This is all wrong.

We're not friends. We're not casual. And we certainly aren't cordial.

We're fire and ice and everything in between.

"I'm rewriting my book," I say with my back still to him.

Closing the door, I turn around and see he's looking up at me. A pen is in his hand, like he was about to get back to working on his friend's arrangement.

They'll have to wait.

"The ending wasn't right, so I'm revising it," I say.

Kent turns to Sydney. "Um, maybe we should come back, let them have their time."

Sydney shushes him. "Are you kidding? Once Jake told us about her, I read her books. I need to know how this one ends."

I can't help the slight laugh that escapes my lips.

Jake leans back on his heels and crosses his arms in front of his body. "Oh yeah?" He seems intrigued. "How does it end this time?"

"Well …" My hands fiddle with the flowers I'm holding. The cellophane crinkles with every push of my fingers. "She walks into his flower shop and buys a bouquet of flowers. Daisies, to be exact, because he once told her they were the best way to show your love." I turn to Kent and Sydney and explain, "They're actually made of two flowers—the yellow middle is one, and the white outer ring is another. Together, they become one."

I take a sure, steady breath and walk closer to Jake. "You see, she was wrong. It's not the longevity of the relationship that makes it more likely for the couple to have true love. It's the depth. It is lust and great sex and witty banter and laughs. It's listening to the other when they open up to you and being there when they need a friend." I step forward. "It's showing up at his place of work and making a complete fool of yourself because you're sorry for acting the way you did."

The air in the room feels ripe with tension as I stare at Jake while his eyes travel over my face, searching for something.

"So, the ending to your book," he says, "she walks into the shop because she knows all of these things, but what does she tell the hero?" He looks to Sydney and winks. "That's me, by the way."

I'd roll my eyes if I wasn't so damn determined to get this guy to realize how serious I was about him. He's not making it easy though.

"She could say …" I pause and swallow, looking up to him. Then, I say with conviction, "I haven't changed my view on if a forever kind of love exists because the past hasn't been kind. However, I can't deny how truly, madly, deeply in love I am with you, and I'm willing to lay it all out and see where this love takes us. Because I'd rather be scared and in your arms than safe and lonely because you're gone."

His mouth rises in a genuine smile as he lays his hands on the counter and asks, "Is that all?"

Jeez, he's not going to let me off at all. I have many more things I should say. A thousand things I feel. But I'm wiser than he thinks.

With a lift of my chin, I say, "Then, she asks him to tell her how he feels. I didn't know what to write, so I thought I'd ask you for some input."

Seeming intrigued, he nods with a grimace as he looks down. "Interesting. You know, she did break his heart pretty bad. Everyone saw how in love she was with him, except for her." He turns to Sydney. "Even her best friend was on his side."

Jake stands tall and slowly walks around the counter. "His sister, however, gave him a task. She told him to read the books. So, he did. He read all of her self-published romances with an open mind, and an open heart."

"You really read them all?" I ask, dumbfounded.

"I did. Well, the hero did, and he's exhausted. Stayed up way too late last night, reading the last one. Turns out, his sister was right. The books were an inside peek into what he'd already known. Your past might have hurt you, but it also built you."

"Then, why didn't he come back home?"

He stands before me, and I tilt my head up as he

gently explains, "It wasn't to be cruel. It was because it's what she needed. She doesn't need a man coming into her life and telling her what she wants. She deserves a man who will let her figure out what she desires on her own."

My heart leaps, and I bite my lip to control my smile. "She desires him. Enough to get all gussied up in a gold dress and do her hair and makeup because she knows he likes the way she looks in that dress."

"He has inappropriate dreams about her in that dress."

"Can we please stop talking in third person?" I ask.

He grins. "Under one condition. Tell me what happens after she professes her love to him."

"He tells her he loves her right back. And then he comes home."

"Lacey?"

"Yes, Jake?"

"I love you right back."

I smile. "Thank God. Because I'm never doing this kind of thing ever again."

His hands snake around my waist as he pulls me in for a kiss. "Fuck that. Your boyfriend is a romantic, the center of your universe. I expect bells and whistles all the time."

I grip his hair and yank him closer. "Maybe."

He leans back, keeping the kiss from my lips.

I relent. "Always."

"Better," he whispers against my lips, pressing into them.

We kiss in a flower shop in the heart of Chicago. We kiss in front of a couple who probably doesn't know what to do with themselves right now. And we kiss for the first time in what will be a very long and devastatingly beautiful love story.

Except this story will never, ever end.

EPILOGUE

This past year has been an absolute whirlwind. After the release of *The Artist,* my sales skyrocketed to levels I hadn't known were possible. I signed the contract with Winston Arms, and the third and final book in my newest series just released.

It's been interesting, not having complete control of the releases like I did in the past, but the publisher has given me opportunities to reach readers outside of my initial fan base. My back catalog sales have tripled, and I'm closing out the year with the best income I've ever had. Plus, my readers, who have been true supporters from the beginning, are beyond happy with the new books. That is the best reward.

Oh, and I made the *New York Times* Best Seller List so that didn't suck.

"You weren't kidding when you said you needed help," Jake says as he carries another box of books over to my table at the book signing we're doing.

"Our girl is a ticketed author now." Charisse nudges me as I grin and sign a paperback for a reader.

Yes, I have both Charisse and Jake assisting me today at the Wisconsin Romance Event. And, yes, I'm a ticketed author. There might be fifty authors at the signing, but two other authors and I have been flagged as hot-ticket authors. I've had readers form lines to see me but never so many that they needed a ticket. It's a bit surreal.

"Why do they need a ticket again?" he asks as he takes a spot next to me.

"Do you see how long this line is? You get a ticket with a number, and when they call your group, you can get in line," Charisse explains.

I glance around the room, seeing the people waiting in line just to meet me. I can't believe it.

I'm so happy to have my two favorite people by my side. With over two hundred preorders and the other hundreds of books I brought, I knew I'd need as much help as possible. We have an assembly line going, where Charisse takes the new orders and Jake finds the preorders.

My life has become everything I ever wanted. I have my dream career, my dream best friend, and even more, my dream boyfriend.

"I'd gladly take a ticket for a minute with this one." Jake kisses my head.

A pretty woman with brightly colored hair steps up to my table with the biggest smile on her face as she grips three of my books close to her chest. "I'm so excited to meet you, Lacey," she says.

"Hi! I'm just as excited to meet you. What's your name?"

She sets her books down, so I can see the name tag she was given when she entered the event. "Oh, sorry, I'm Trudy."

"Do you live around here?"

"I do. And I was so glad when I heard you were coming to Milwaukee. You're my unicorn author, and I never thought I'd get the chance to meet you."

"Aw, thank you for enjoying my books. And, yes, this was an easy signing for me to attend, as I only live a little over an hour away." I pick up the books she put on the table and start signing each one with a quote from the novel.

She makes a gasping sound, and I look up to see if she's okay.

"This is him, right? This is Jake? The man you used as a muse for *The Artist*?" she asks, nodding her head and pointing toward Jake, who stands taller, making sure she sees his shirt.

Yes, he is very proud of the shirt he had made that says, *Her Inspiration*, across the front of it. I can't help but laugh when I notice him showing it off like a damn peacock.

"I see you follow my social media," I say as I raise a brow to Charisse.

She's made it her job to share as much of my and Jake's real-life love story on my Instagram as she can get away with. I had to hold her back on using a photo she'd found on my phone of a naked florist in a hot tub.

Jake takes the opportunity to lean forward to reach his hand out to shake Trudy's, who visibly swoons at his

Colgate smile and soft-as-satin touch. I turn to Charisse, who laughs as I roll my eyes in fake annoyance.

The truth is, I love how comfortable he is in his own skin. It makes me feel better in my own. Our lives even blend together so easily. I write while he's at work, and we spend every free minute exploring the city or curling up on the couch, watching a chick flick. We hang out with Charisse and Melody as a couple at least once a week, and he has introduced me to half of Chicago since he seems to know someone everywhere we go. I still need my space though, so I partake in my weekly girls' night and have coffee with my mother. If I'm on a deadline, I'll park myself at Starbucks for a few hours. Jake says he hates being apart, but I think the space makes him want me more, so it's a win-win.

I hand Trudy back her books and take a photo with her before saying good-bye and welcoming other readers.

I have my head turned, taking a quick sip of water when, to my surprise, I see my mom standing in front of my table, carrying my most recent book.

"Mom?" I ask, not sure if I'm seeing things clearly.

She grins from ear to ear.

"What are you doing here? Why are you in line?" I ask, looking around like I'm missing something.

She beams with pride. "I'm here to have my daughter's book signed." She hands it to me.

"I could have signed it anytime for you. You didn't have to drive all this way, and you certainly didn't have to wait in line. My goodness, how long have you been waiting?"

She shrugs. "I wanted to experience the signing.

Someone"—she points a finger toward Jake—"thought it might be good for me to witness the fandom for myself. I must admit, hearing the chatter around me of how moved people are by your prose has made it all worth it. It has been … quite an eye-opener."

"Really?"

"You've always been brilliant. I'm just so proud of how many people you've touched with your words."

I stand up with tears in my eyes and wrap my arms around her. "I love you, Mom."

She hugs me back just as tightly. "You should be very proud of what you've created and who you've become. I know I am."

As I step back, I wipe the tear falling from my eye. I'd be remiss if I didn't give my mom a little credit for the success of the new series with Winston Arms. Complex issues and real-world troubles are woven into these stories. They have heart—and not the overly fanciful kind. It's the kind that makes you believe that not only does love exist, but inner peace too. My mom showed me that was possible.

"Here, let me take a picture of the two of you," Charisse says, holding up my phone and motioning to the both of us.

We stand next to each other with huge smiles covering our faces.

I ask her to stay and hang out with us, and before long she's assisting Jake with the preorders, becoming a great addition to our team. Every once in a while, my mom walks over and rubs my back—her silent way of saying how proud she is of me.

After the signing, we pack up and then exchange

pleasantries with the other authors. Mom and Charisse both want to get home at a decent time, so I take the very small box of books we have left after the signing and load it into Charisse's car to bring back to Chicago before they bid me and Jake goodnight.

When they're both safe and driving away from the hotel, I turn to Jake, who runs his hands up and down my arms.

"Are you sure you don't want to go home too?" I ask him.

He takes my hand and pulls me into the lobby. "And miss a night in a hotel room with the sexiest woman in publishing? Never."

"Yes, but you could have a night in the wonderful house in Lincoln Park." My attempt to persuade him to go home fails.

"My mother is still shocked I convinced you to move in with me."

"I didn't just move in. We bought a house. You do realize what this means for my fear-of-failing-relationships heart?"

He pulls me close and kisses me firmly. "That you know this one isn't going anywhere." His words are spoken against my lips.

I grin with a shake of my head and follow him into the elevator.

I'm amazed we still want to be with each other every waking moment since we bought the house a month ago. Moving in wasn't a big deal for us, as we'd basically lived together already. Living next door to one another made it hard to go home. It was just a matter of whose bed we were sleeping in each night.

The first night we had attempted staying at our own places for the night ended with him trying to talk in Morse code through our thin walls. It was cute for a little while, but it only made me want him lying next to me more. A half hour later, we were making love on my living-room floor.

Our leases were up for renewal around the same time. That was when Jake floated the idea about buying a place of our own. I was thinking we'd get a bigger apartment. He had grander ideas. The house is a gorgeous Tudor in upscale Lincoln Park and way more home than I have ever had. I was hesitant and about to say *no way* until he showed me my office. With built-in bookcases and a picture window overlooking the backyard … I was intrigued. When he told me his idea to have a reading nook built under the slanted eaves … I was sold.

He had a designer come in and work with the two of us to combine our styles. His high-end with my wine-stained one seem to blend together quite nicely.

While I love my house, I'm content with sleeping anywhere as long as Jake's there.

God, I'm such a sap.

And I love it!

He slides the key card into the door, and we walk into our suite at the Milwaukee Regent. I run to the bed and plop down on it, lying with my arms out wide.

The emotions and feelings running through my body are always intense after signings. It's like a huge crash from the highest of highs. I was a ball of nerves before, convinced no one would show. Then, they showed, and I was anxious not to disappoint them. I kept a smile and stayed on point for hours, talking to hundreds of people until my throat hurt. My nerves were kept tight, and now that it's all over, it's like a whoosh of energy leaving my body. I just want to crash. So, I am. Into the fine thread count of this very fancy bed.

Jake walks over to his suitcase and pulls out a bottle of my favorite cabernet. "Shall I open it?" he asks with a shit-eating grin on his face.

I hold up my arm in the air with my thumb held high as my answer.

He laughs as he taunts, "Come on. You're okay. You weren't *that* busy at the signing."

I sit up straight in shock. "Not that busy? My wrist has a cramp, which, for the record, I am not complaining about! I just can't believe how long some people waited in that line. I remember being that reader, waiting to see E.L. James and Colleen Hoover." I close my eyes, still not able to fully digest how enormous this all was.

Jake sits next to me on the bed, handing me a glass of wine. "You've had an amazing year, and readers are literally lining up to read your books."

I laugh and hit his stomach with the back of my hand at his little joke. Then, my smile fades because as happy as I am, I'll always feel hesitant in my gut.

"It scares me. The success," I confess. "The bigger I get, the more people to disappoint."

"Well, that's true. You're always going to have critics. There's also more people to inspire."

I stare into his gorgeous brown eyes. "You always know the right thing to say."

He kisses my lips and then pulls back. "You don't give yourself enough credit."

I smile brightly. "What did I ever do to deserve you?"

I lean in to kiss him again, making sure he knows just how much I cherish him. When he pulls back, his grin shows he knows what I meant.

"You knocked on my door and yelled at me for playing music too loudly." He squeezes my leg and then stands to walk to the table that has the room service menu. "What do you say we blow off our reservations for tonight, stay in, and order one of everything on the menu?" He raises his eyebrows in my direction.

"As long as everything includes a cheeseburger with a brownie for dessert, then I say, that's a plan."

"One cheeseburger and a brownie coming up!" He picks up the phone to place the order.

"Really? You're okay with staying in tonight and not exploring the city? I thought you had a friend who had a friend who owned a restaurant."

"Tonight's your night. If you're exhausted and you want to relax, then that's what we'll do. Funny how the nights in become much more fun than nights out. Plus, I packed a seafoam-green towel I plan to model for you."

If I didn't already love this man, his ability to compromise would have me swooning hard for him.

We had plans to eat at a super-fancy restaurant he had been looking forward to, so I'll make it up to him another night. For now, nothing sounds better than taking a hot bath and lying around in Jake's arms for the rest of the night. After he models that seafoam-green towel, of course.

When I wake up, it's to an empty bed. I glance around and find Jake standing next to the window, staring out at the beautiful view around us, as the sun peeks through the curtains.

"How long have you been awake?" I ask as I stretch.

He turns, and I see the long-stemmed rose in his hand.

He slowly makes his way over to me. "Since five."

"Five? Why? Go back to sleep," I say, pulling the covers up closer and telling myself the same thing.

"I can't. I had a dream."

"Everything okay?" I ask sleepily.

"It was a revelation." He sounds so prophetic.

I open my eyes and tilt my head in question when he continues, *"You said, 'We don't get to choose our family. We only get to choose who we love.' You were wrong."*

I blink my eyes, wondering if I'm still asleep because those words sound very familiar, like I've heard them before. I definitely didn't say them to him though. It doesn't make sense to my sleep-fogged brain.

Before I can ask for clarification, he continues again, *"I didn't choose to love you. This love chose me. It hit me like a ton of bricks. It seeped into my skin every second since until my entire body was consumed. It's brilliant and scary as hell."*

My eyes open wide as I realize what he's doing. These *are* my words. Not from my mouth. They're words from one of my books, and he's reciting them back to me.

Sitting up, I stare at him, bewildered. "How do you have my quotes memorized like that?"

His mega-watt grin shines as he takes a step toward the bed.

"I choose you. I want a life with you. I want you by my side, I want to live this life with you. Fight with you. Make love to you. Create life with you," he says with a soulful purpose to his words.

I tilt my head, confused and honored at the same time when something dawns on me, making me gasp and cover my mouth in surprise.

My heart stops as everything he said sinks in. That was the speech my hero gave in one of my books before he proposed to the heroine.

I shake my head and look down at the duvet, convinced I'm misreading the situation when I realize the other two lines he recited are from other proposal scenes in my books.

"Jake," I says, hesitantly. "What are you doing?"

My breath hitches because my heart is racing wildly, surprising me with how badly it wants my hunch to be true.

He sits down on the bed beside me, leans in, and whispers, *"I choose you for eternity."*

Our lips meet and I absolutely melt into him.

My lids are still hooded as he pulls back and adds, "Now, get up. I have a day planned for us."

"But—"

He places his finger over my mouth, silencing me and shaking his head. "Let's get ready first."

I fling off the sheets and rush to the bathroom, ready to get dressed for the day, glad I brought a dress I know he loves.

My hair is blown out, and I add a touch of lipstick. Once I have my shoes on, I'm ready to go. I stand by the door with a smile on my face, waiting to see what he says, but he only grabs my hand and leads me out of the room.

After we hop in the car, he heads to the Milwaukee Art Museum as it's somewhere he said he wanted to see while we were in town. We tour the displays and enjoy the morning of enrichment and each other's company. I almost forget his reciting of my fictional proposals as we stroll down the halls.

Once we're walking out of the museum, hand in hand, he turns to me and says, *"I am wildly, crazily, passionately in love with you. I don't just love you. I live for you."*

I smile big as he pauses and holds out his free hand, where I see he has notes written on a tiny piece of paper. I recognize the words to this one immediately. It's from my friends-to-lovers romance.

When he looks back to me, it's with a smile when he sees my face, and I know what he's doing. It doesn't stop him though.

"You're the only woman I have ever and will ever love. I lost you once, and I will never lose you again. That's why I'm not asking; I'm telling you."

My heart squeezes as I wait for the next words because, in the book, they were, *Will you marry me?*

He leans in to kiss me sweetly, and when he pulls back, he says, "I'm telling you, I love you."

I squint my eyes at him, and he lets out a small chuckle before pulling my hand as he steps away and heads back to the car. I play with the hem of my dress and smash my lips, wondering what on earth he's up to.

He drives to our next place, a cute little diner, where

we order at a counter and then make our way to a table in the corner.

I stare at him, waiting for whatever he's going to say next, but he just goes about with his day, acting like he hasn't recited two proposals from my books. Nope, he talks about the museum and what he liked the most as well as the signing and how amazed he was with the attendance and how many books I'd sold.

I'm dying here, waiting for him to finish his thought, and I know he's enjoying keeping me on the line like this.

We eat our food, and I try not to think about what's going on in his mind, but it's killing me on the inside.

As we walk to the car after lunch, he stops at my door and pushes me up against it. When he leans down to kiss me, my heart pounds, and my knees go weak. He holds me up, deepening our kiss, and I melt in his arms.

As he pulls back, he places his finger on my cheek as he says, *"I never thought love was in the cards for me. The idea of having a partner in life was so foreign to me that I never even considered the option. My life was complete until you came along."*

I smile brightly. This one's from my single-dad rock-star book.

"You are more than a partner though. You've become my other half—the other half of my heart, the other part of my world. My family loves you just as much as I do. You've made our family complete, yet there's still one thing missing." He pauses, and I look into his eyes as he continues to recite the lines from the book, *"Do you know what's missing?"*

"Me taking your name," I respond. Although, in the book, it actually says, *You taking my name*, but I wanted to change it up for us.

He shakes his head. "Nope. What's missing are the ones we love."

I take a sharp inhale, questioning everything and wondering what's going on in that head of his.

He opens the car door and nudges me to sit down and pull my feet in.

"Are you trying to torture me?" I finally ask. "Because if you are, you're succeeding."

He laughs, kissing me again. "I have no idea what you're talking about."

Jake winks, and I let out a huff, crossing my arms over my chest. He closes the door, and when he enters on his side, he starts it and then grabs my hand to hold as he drives to our next destination.

A sign on the road reads, *McKinley Beach*. When we get out, I see a group of people close to the water, and as we approach them, I realize who's all here.

Everyone we love.

His entire family is here along with my mom, Charisse, and Melody. Sweet Aubrey runs to me when she sees us from afar.

"Auntie," she yells as I pick her up.

"Hello, my sweet baby girl. What's going on here?" I ask as I tickle her tummy and try to get some info out of her.

"Oh no, you don't," Charisse says. "She has strict orders not to say anything to you but hello. We knew you'd try to trick her."

I laugh as I hug Charisse and then Melody.

"Have you guys been here the entire time?" I ask Melody.

She shrugs. "We had fun at the hotel pool while you guys were at the signing yesterday."

I say hello to everyone, giving them all hugs and loving the feeling of family I get from every single person here. When I get to Bobbi, her eyes are brimmed with tears, and they only make me fight back my own.

When I turn back to Jake, it's to him on his knee, holding out a gorgeous diamond ring.

"Lacey, I've read your stories of hopeless people finding love and of people who fought off ideas of ever finding *the one*. I've loved being your muse, but nothing is as good as being by your side. You write some pretty amazing couples, but they will never beat us. Because your heroines will never be you. They'll never have your charm, your drive, or your love. I've enjoyed every second I've been with you since the moment you kissed me for a damn TikTok challenge. I knew right then that you were different and exactly what I wanted in my life. So, Lacey Wampo, will you marry me?"

I leap over to him, almost tackling him to the ground, screaming, "Yes!"

Everyone cheers as he stands us up and hugs me tightly.

"I love you, Lacey," he whispers into my ear as he runs his hand through my hair, holding me tighter to him.

"I love you more," I say as tears fall down my face. "Thank you for breaking my writer's block and making my life complete."

NAUGHTY NEIGHBOR

He pulls back and smiles big at me before kissing my lips in front of everyone we love. They hoot and holler in celebration with us for finding each other and a love that will last a lifetime.

BEFORE YOU GO…

Do you want to keep up with Jeannine and Lauren as well as sign up for a chance to receive a zodiac themed surprise care package in the mail? Sign up below to be entered!

https://bit.ly/2E6A584

The next book in the Falling for the Stars series, CHARMING COWORKER (FALLING FOR A SAGITTARIUS), releases November 23, 2020. Preorder your copy now!

https://amzn.to/35A0UfZ

Ready to read the books Lacey was writing in Naughty Neighbor? Check out THE SEXTON BROTHERS SERIES—AUSTIN, BRYCE AND TANNER—by Jeannine and Lauren that are out now as a box set and in KU!

https://amzn.to/2QySTjE

ACKNOWLEDGMENTS

When we were writing the last book in the Sexton Brothers series, *Tanner*, Lauren became obsessed with the song *Him and I* by G-Easy & Halsey, especially because of the music video and how much it reminded her of Tanner and Harper.

In the song there's a lyric that says, *Only one who gets me, I'm a crazy fuckin' Gemini.*

That's when the idea hit us. Whether you believe it or not, everyone knows their zodiac sign and celebrates their unique characteristics because of it. The idea for twelve books was born and, after we finished the Sexton Brothers and some solo projects, we jumped in, ready to write the books together.

Such a series is quite the undertaking, but we knew we could do it with the help of our wonderful PA, Autumn Gantz with Wordsmith Publicity. We can't thank you enough for guiding us through and making sure we were on track while we had our heads in each book.

A huge thank you to Wilmari Carrasquillo-Delgado and Chelle Lagoski Northcutt for being our beta readers.

Our books wouldn't be what they are today without the help of Jovana Shirley with Unforeseen Editing. It blows our minds the things she's able to spot and make sure the book flows for consistency. We're so grateful for Allisia Wysong also for helping us with a quick proofread!

And of course, we can never thank our readers enough. Without you guys we wouldn't be able to follow our dreams and have our daily conversations from different sides of the United States. We found our friendship through books, and get to continue due to your support.

Thank you!

ABOUT THE AUTHORS

Jeannine Colette

Jeannine Colette is the author of the Abandon Collection – a series of stand-alone novels featuring dynamic heroines who have to abandon their reality in order to discover themselves . . . and love along the way. Each book features a new couple, exciting new city and a rose of a different color.

A graduate of Wagner College and the New York Film Academy, Jeannine went on to become a Segment Producer for television shows on CBS and NBC. She left the television industry to focus on her children and pursue a full-time writing career. She lives in New York with her husband, the three tiny people she adores more than life itself, and a rescue pup named Wrigley.

Want to hear about new releases and get exciting emails from me? Sign up for my monthly newsletter!

www.jeanninecolette.com/newsletter

WWW.JEANNINECOLETTE.COM

Check out her books on Goodreads:
https://bit.ly/2r3Z9RJ

Follow her:
Facebook: www.facebook.com JeannineColetteBooks/
Twitter: www.twitter.com/JeannineColett
Instagram: www.instagram.com/jeanninecolette/
BookBub: www.bookbub.com/authors/jeannine-colette
BookandMain: www.bookandmainbites.com/JeannineColette

Join her Facebook group: JCol's Army of Roses

Lauren Runow

Lauren Runow is the author of multiple Adult Contemporary Romance novels, some more dirty than others. When Lauren isn't writing, you'll find her listening to music, at her local CrossFit, reading, or at the baseball field with her boys. Her only vice is coffee, and she swears it makes her a better mom!

Lauren is a graduate from the Academy of Art in San Francisco and is the founder and co-owner of the community magazine she and her husband publish. She is a proud Rotarian, helps run a local non-profit kids science museum, and was awarded Woman of the Year from Congressman Garamendi. She lives in Northern California with her husband and two sons.

You can also stay in touch through the social media links below.

www.LaurenRunow.com

Sign up for her newsletter at http://bit.ly/2NEXgH1

Check out her books on Goodreads:
http://bit.ly/1Isw3Sv

Follow her on:
Facebook at www.facebook.com/laurenjrunow
Instagram at www.instagram.com/Lauren_Runow/
BookBub at www.bookbub.com/authors/lauren-runow
Twitter at www.twitter.com/LaurenRunow
BookandMain: www.bookandmainbites.com/
LaurenRunow

Join her reader group on Facebook: Lauren's Law
Breakers

Made in the USA
Middletown, DE
15 September 2023

38332980R00172